THE NOTARY

Tartaria

Hector Omar Aldana

TABLE OF CONTENTS

PREFACE

GEO'S COMA

Late one evening, Geo is on a beach in the Yucatan with his 5-year-old daughter, Summer. As the sun sets below the horizon, suddenly, a comet shoots across the starlit sky! In awe, Summer looks at Geo with excitement in her eyes. She traces the comet's wake and notices three bright stars in its path. Mesmerized, she asks, "Daddy, what is that?" Geo takes her hand and directs her finger to connect the stars of Orion's belt. Summer sees the shape and whispers, "Daddy, look, I'm connecting the dots!"

Geo and Summer connect the dots of all the bright stars and find more constellations. Together, they trace all the constellations in the zodiac as Geo explains the myths of the gods and the secrets they reveal. Geo says, "Summer, when you connect all the dots you will touch the sky." Summer beams at Geo, smiling at her handsome father in the starlight as the vivid dream comes to a sudden traumatic flash and end.

Suddenly Geo finds himself harshly awakened and saved from an induced lucid coma of an endearing moment with his daughter. An aging Chinese man dressed in a grey robe by the name of Li Mi Chen found a distressed Geo in the back-alley way near the Lipo bar in Chinatown, San Francisco, where he was drugged and beat by a fierce Triad gang. Recently Geo's life has become unstable, and he lost sight of his beautiful daughter, who gives his life meaning. She is his everything.

Geo has child support and alimony payments and dwindling reserves. Yet, he will see his daughter Summer again. Geo vows to provide for his daughter as he carves out of thin air a new life and meaning for both of them.

CHAPTER 1

MÉNAGE À TRIOS

Late one hot summer evening, Geo walks into his average suburban ranch home in an average suburban neighborhood, with average suburban neighbors, after a long day at the brokerage firm where he is a Partner. That morning, September 29, 2008, the market imploded, now etched in American minds in infamy. Many lost their equities, businesses, and homes to foreclosure.

The secondary lending market B-paper backed with bad credit started to default. Real estate mortgage terms reset to higher interest rates covertly embedded within each adjustable loan program. Homeowners signed at low teaser interest rates, eager to live the American dream to own a home. But since the rates rose overnight, owners had no means to pay the dramatic increase in their monthly mortgage payments and hefty prepayment penalties. Worse, most never read the obscene loan terms they agreed to.

Massive defaults shocked mortgage companies and banks, causing a domino effect on prime mortgage loans. In days, real estate market values began to plummet, driving every industry and stock price associated with the real estate industry to plunge simultaneously. Homeowners were stuck with homes with lower market values than their loan amounts. The excessive prepayment penalties trapped homeowners defrauded by the loan terms, causing a colossal home foreclosure fiasco that would take years to undo.

To avoid a meltdown of the American banking system, the Federal Reserve went on a borrowing spree that added trillions of dollars of never-ending debt to the current Federal Reserve banking system and national debt.

As Geo helplessly connected the dots that led to the 2008

real estate market crash, he called it the "Banking Cartel." Several years before, The democratic President signed the Gramm-Leach-Bliley Act, which repealed the 1933 depression era Glass-Steagall Act that created the FDIC and kept banks, lenders, and Wall Street stock brokers from colluding and comingling profits with insurance companies to keep the public safe from bad investments.

The corrupt democratic president who was recently accused of receiving fellatio in the Whitehouse and his lobby sugar-coated the Gramm-Leach-Bliley Act to provide consumer privacy to be a safe lending mechanism for Americans to thrive financially, yet cloaked in semantics to only benefit the Banking Cartel into the next market crash.

When the dust cleared a decade later, millions of people lost jobs, unemployment soared, and corporations bought foreclosed properties at pennies on the dollar. The entire fiasco reminded Geo of Pleasure Island when Pinocchio and the "Stupid Little Boys' were enticed by the mischievous Coachman with candy. Yet when the timing was right, the stupid little boys turned into laughable wild donkeys. They took the Coachman's temptation and paid for it dearly.

All the slick, sharp-suited Partners at the firm were gripping their plush leather armchairs over the breaking news unfolding on giant TV screens in their posh conference room as Geo tried to explain how, what, and why the crash was happening. All their lives were about to change. Everyone left the office late that evening in disheveled emotional disarray.

The market crash was the beginning of the end of Geo's real estate career. His life savings was gone. Since his youth, real estate was the only profession he knew. He had no other skills but being a real estate agent.

The tragic event left an internal scar in Geo that ironically led him to spiritual epiphanies and to rebuild his future, set up in divine providence and that would soon take place.

On that very day, Geo drives home feeling like he was living a surreal nightmare. He parked his car in the garage and was speechless for a few minutes. His mind was void of thought. He didn't know what to say to his wife Nadia.

Nadia was originally from Cuba, educated at a UC state college, and when they married, she chose to be a homemaker to raise their family. Geo had a life of success and no failures until this point. Briefcase in hand, as he walked into his home, the halogen track lights in the living room were dim. Geo heard voices echoing from the hallway. As he approached his half-opened bedroom door, a man was having aggressive sex with his wife, Nadia. Geo's first thought was a home invasion as the man was raping his wife. Maybe he had entered the wrong home? And in that split second, he ran out of excuses, and reality set in. Like a movie, he quietly watched as his precious beautiful wife deeply moaned as silky beads of sweat rolled down her fine back to her ass as this strange tall blond man had his way with her.

She was so beautiful, yet her lust turned against Geo that very second. As Geo peered further into the bedroom to inspect the current proceeding of things, he saw what he thought was the man's tanned reflection in the mirror. But no, it was another naked male receiving fellatio from Nadia as she posed horizontally between both men with Nadia in the middle of the California king bed they shared. Two men standing there with their eyes feverishly shut as they gripped Nadia by the head and ankles, working on her deep as Geo frantically watched them do this to his wife! His briefcase slipped from his hand in shock and made no sound when it hit the floor amid the moaning in the human-heated room.

As Geo's heartbeat was in a rhythm of suspended belief, none of the participants noticed him voyeuristically and reluctantly listening and watching every move in that room. For those moments, the entire lewd scene morphed from a threesome into a foursome as Geo's aura was sucked from his body to voyeuristically reluctantly participate as an uninvited ghost in this insidious event as two men groped and fondled his wife like feverish wild animals. Geo was unseated as this out of body experience continued.

The mere 30 seconds was an eternity for Geo. The ruckus of the bed's metal legs banging on the dark oakwood hardwood floor as Nadia's deep moans melted like butter on a bun he never heard come from within her before. His senses started to cave in and shut down.

It was as if his anguished spirit jumped back into his body and became one again with him. He snapped out of the trance and took a few steps back as Geo frantically ran back out into the backyard where he lay curled up, hidden by the swimming pool in the dark where no one could find him as he watched the swimming pool still, calm water flow down the waterfall for hours and hours until time stopped for him. The image of the betrayal threesome was etched hard into Geo's heart, mind, and soul.

Geo's defenses were worn and shut, and he had no fight left in him on that given day. He was withdrawn and locked into emotional and spiritual submission, although he never practiced religion. Earlier that day, Nadia thought Geo was supposed to go out to dinner with the other partners at the firm later that evening. Still, she didn't count on the uneventful real estate market crashing earlier that day, so Nadia didn't plan on Geo's early arrival at their home. Nadia had always been a lousy scheduler of events. When the two gentlemen were done and left their home, Nadia found Geo's brown leather briefcase perfectly hard and erect, standing there lonely by itself near the bedroom door, and the truth of what she had done immediately set into her.

Geo lay by the pool all night long, saddened by the harsh unbelievable things he had just witnessed in disbelief. His career was crashing. His marriage to the wife he loved crashed too. Soon the entire life he had built with his wife since they met in college came crashing down in every which direction. Geo met the reality of his financially egotistical life, a future built on a frivolous, seemingly strong foundation no one could predict was defective and would eventually crumble into the past.

CHAPTER 2

NADIA – FIDEL CASTRO'S CREATION

Nadia was a long-haired brunette, short but fit with firm legs from her love of Cuban salsa dancing. She had breast augmentation and a defined jawline that gave her exotic eyes appeal. Her soft but smaller clef chin made her even more attractive and gave her an overall sexy allure. Yet when she spoke, her Cuban accent put men into overdrive and made them lose their sense of control. Men acted like wild Billy goats anytime she passed by in her tight skirts, dresses, and heels. Geo would always hold her by the hand as a couple, not because he was jealous, but because other men would lose control over their boundaries when she was present. So, both agreed to act as a singular unit to avoid altercations for undiscerning ignorant men who lost their ability to think clearly and respectfully around her. Nadia was a sexy, beautiful woman with a cultural Cuban femininity she could not resist being.

Geo met Nadia in an accidental collision with her at the student union during a college protest that had gone out of control. He was headed to the student union to get some lunch, unaware of the protest, as she was running away from the campus police, who were spraying water and mace at the students protesting The Maleconazo. The Maleconazo was a protest on 5 August 1994, in which thousands of Cubans took to the streets around the Malecón in Havana to demand freedom and express frustration with the government, and in support, so did the Cuban students in America.

As Geo turned the corner, Nadia, running in high heels, tripped over her best friend Bobby, and landed on Geo, knocking them both to the ground as Geo padded Nadia's fall with himself. Bobby took off running back to the protest leaving Geo and Nadia on the ground. Geo gathered himself to surmise what was happening with the protesters as Nadia screamed, "Hide me!"

Like the rest of the men, Geo could not resist her beauty and instantly devised a plan for a quick getaway with her through the student union halls and a back door to safety. Geo felt very fortunate for this very unfortunate rendezvous. As they urgently walked out of the campus, Nadia stumbled along with one semi-broken heel, but Geo still felt his stomach grumbling and could not believe that he had just helped this piercing exotic girl with runny eyeliner. Geo was a bit nervous about being around her; she was too beautiful for him. He mustered a bit of inner strength as they walked together and laughed about their encounter and the protest. He took a leap of faith and asked if she wanted to eat Chinese food at Ming's restaurant a few blocks North of the campus. To Geo's surprise, Nadia invited him to her apartment instead. Of course, he could not resist that Spanish Cuban accent and agreed again. As they reached her apartment, Nadia excused herself to take a quick shower and few moments later came out of the bedroom wearing a black lace silk chemise silhouetted by the living room light revealing her physique. Geo could see her shapely small marshmallow-like nipples and firm, altered breasts through the lace.

Geo spontaneously said, "You look very beautiful." Nadia offhandedly responded, "Cuban women dress more seductively than American women; it's our culture. Nadia had a very peering look as she spoke, looking straight into Geo's eyes. There was nothing to hide from her.

She microwaved some pulled pork meat from her refrigerator she had cooked earlier and grilled some cheesy pork sandwiches for two using artisan French bread. They ate and shared a glass of cheap red wine together that only college students could afford. They didn't say a word but smiled at each other as they ate. She took out a red leather box filled with green leafy square sheets of what appeared to be fermented tobacco leaves and curly shavings and started rolling a handmade cigar. She poured the shavings on top of each tobacco leaf and rolled them passionately, taking care to smooth the roll with incremental amounts of the tobacco shavings measured to the precise angle of each fermented tobacco sheet. Each cigar appeared to be phallic in size, which Geo found erotic as Nadia skillfully rolled each with her long-defined fingers.

Geo found this act exciting and peculiar, as if Nadia had a masculine side, expressed vividly when she confidently licked each cigar with her unusually long tongue, wrapped in her saliva and plush lips. Nadia said her twin cousins Ernesto and Enrique smuggled all the ingredients straight from Cuba, therefore the cigars were as authentic as her to be smoked.

Geo was curious about Cuba. Nadia came from a city named Santa Clara. During Castro's and Che's takeover, two types of Cubans last until this day. One type learned not to trust Castro and loathe his tyrannical regime. And the other type of Cuban supports all of his socialistic Marxist ideologies even when they escape to America because they have little hope for the poor and are poor, ironically. This type of Cuban tends to vote for progressive legislation in America that constantly contradicts the US Constitution and amendments, and, somehow ironically, they believe in the quintessential American dream. Nadia had always worn a precious silver diamond-encrusted Star of David necklace to signify to others that she was Jewish. It turned out that Nadia and Nadia's family were the Jewish type that supported the Castro regime in every way, even in America. Yet, they fell straight into the American Leftist political schemes in how they voted politically. Nadia and her family migrated from Cuba to Israel. Then they found their way into the United States because it was easier to legally immigrate from Israel than from Cuba and because they had become Jewish and had Jewish American connections to come into America. Sometimes, they escaped from Cuba in tiny handmade floating junk boats. While many perished at sea, it seemed to Geo, the survivors merely wished to create another tyrannical socialist Cuba in America. Although Geo was young and uninterested and uninformed and a bit immature at that point. He had no opinion as he was not into Jews, socialism, world or American politics, protesting, or worldly events. But he was utterly focused and interested sexually and curiously in Nadia as a young man. Nadia handed him a freshly rolled cigar. She brandished a shiny black-chrome metal guillotine from the leather storage box, which even King Henry VIII would marvel at. She asked Geo to put the tip of the cigar under the guillotine's blade, and in a violent quick-cutting actuation without remorse, she chopped off the tip. It frightened Geo for a moment. She pulled out a brass Victorian-style gas lighter and lit his and her cigars as they both took deep consensual puffs. Although Geo coughed through the thick heavy smoke a few times. They inhaled and exhaled as the drifting cigar smoke lingered in Nadia's apartment. It smelled and tasted sweet to Geo in a strange smokey robust bittersweet way and stung the tip of his tongue like light spicy chilly. Both content and satisfied, Geo reached out his arm, rubbed his index finger on Nadia's chin clef, and gently walked her chin close to his. Their lips met passionately, they kissed, and their tongues lashed sexually entwined with each breath. Geo had fallen in lust with Nadia that day. Innocently thinking it was love throughout his eight-year marriage with her when they married years later.

It was Geo's genetic fallacy as a man, not to see who she was as a person, her upbringing, her values, her family values, and her beliefs. Still, she stroked his ego as a man and womanly sex object. He had no idea that women could possess strong ideological and political personalities of their own, as he lusted his sexuality for her, even though they met in a knockdown collision during a protest that she vehemently believed in. Geo missed the point of why she was protesting and could have gained much insight into who she really was and what she truly believed in had he took the time to get to learn about her intrinsically.

Geo was oblivious as a young man and as a husband to her. Being from Cuba, a third-world nation where daily safety needs, survival, and basic necessities was their prime objective on Maslow's hierarchy of needs. All Nadia needed was a man who represented financial security and a man who would be a good provider for her. Any man that had established that fundamental necessity and value would have and could become her husband, despite who the man was. She didn't fall in love with Geo because of Geo. All Geo represented was her provider.

Was it Geo's unfortunate luck to have collided with her that evening, eventually leading to their marriage? In reality, they were two different people meant for two different meanings and reasons in life, both conflicting with each other eventually. Many years later, Geo found refuge in the fact that everything went wrong between Nadia and him because of their different fundamental reasoning, thinking, and logic. So as long as Geo provided for her, she could have lived in marriage until they both parted from life. Both living seemingly good lives on the surface but a shallow married life devoid of meaning. She had no absolute love for Geo, nor did Geo for her, although they were both highly attracted to each other, and that is what kept their marriage in place until they had their child Summer. As Geo grew to know Nadia, he believed that he had married the wrong person. Geo always put himself in a fantastical mental scenario in his married life, testing their strength together. He would imagine if both of them were on a ship out at sea caught in a storm that was flooding the boat and drowning, he questioned how Nadia would react, and he could not imagine her saving him and putting herself aside for him in one last test of love. Although Geo thought to himself that he would sacrifice his life for her merely as a chivalrous man, not for loving her. At the same time, Geo saw nothing chivalrous about Nadia's loyalty to him. He did not trust Nadia in a deeper state of love. They were very different in fundamental ways.

Geo was not interested in Nadia's explanation or opinion as he was always a serious man of black-and-white decisions, never being caught in grey areas. In those unfaithful moments, he severed Nadia from his life, mind, and heart. He never went back to his home and left everything behind.

The unfortunate betrayal left an internal scar on Geo

that helped lead him to conclusions about future events. The only thing that mattered now was his daughter, Summer. Fortunately, she spent a few weeks with her grandparents during summer break shielding her of what had transpired. Fundamentally, Summer was Geo's driving force in life. He loved his daughter immensely and unconditionally. Nothing will ever account for all the love and experiences, time that Geo and Summer spent together as father and daughter. When Summer was born, he did the honors of carefully severing Nadia's and Summer umbilical during labor and that marked the beginning of his commitment and responsibility to his newly born daughter. Geo's devotion to Summer had no limits, but now all this was about to change.

CHAPTER 3

CHINATOWN

Geo learned one thing that evening. The contrived financial disasters in modern history, like the Great Depression and The Panic of 1907, also known as the Knickerbocker Crisis, proved to be fabricated crashes. Where did all the money come from? And why would money be lent so feverishly by lenders abandoning all traditional lending guidelines? The previous market crashes were contrived, but the 2008 crash marked the true north path for a dystopian future in American lives. It was the beginning of the end of the idea of Freedom in America, yet it impacted the whole world. There was nowhere else left to flee. It was the ultimate control of human life, mirroring tyrannical governments throughout history.

Geo recalls his humanities instructor, Mrs. Rice, a short, unassuming gray-haired lady in her 40s who had a goofy yet intelligent side to her. She was found dead, splattered between a king-size mattress and a sidewalk after the bed flew off the top of a delivery truck striking Mrs. Rice like a rocket as she jogged after work, crushing her like a salami sandwich, kicking her to the literal curb.

Mrs. Rice required each student to read books on authoritarian governments aloud in class as if she was indoctrinating every student to a future they did not yet understand or had prepared for in their upbringing.

They had no idea how history played such an essential role in people's lives. Some of the books were Fahrenheit 451 by Ray Bradbury, The Jungle by Upton Sinclair, 1984 by George Orwell, and movies like The Zeitgeist by Murdock, D.M.; Joseph, Peter and the underlying meanings of books like The Wonderful Wizard of Oz by Lyman Frank Baum, The Creature from Jekyll Island by Edward Griffin, the tyranny of the Federal Reserve by Brian O' Brian, not to mention the diary of Ann Frank. Books that went way beyond the standard required high school curriculum, eventually getting Mrs. Rice in trouble with the school Principal.

Now at this very moment, Geo figured out that Mrs. Rice had a purpose in his life because things suddenly started to make sense. Mrs. Rice planted seeds of wisdom into Geo's mind to carve out his understanding of his placement on this earth. Mrs. Rice was preparing him and a generation of students to ask questions to think logically, question authority, connect the dots, and not trust governments. It all made sense for Geo as his tragic workday ended. It was the crash that everyone highly anticipated, and finally had come home to roost. Yet everyone was skeptical of the newfound wealth in equity and how the value of homes suspiciously rose overnight, and how people were dashing to refinance their homes and using their homes as mini equity banks to support their materialist dreams in buying boats, high fashion, sports cars, named branded suits and dresses and overpriced toys for their children. All of a sudden, everyone had money. Everyone overleveraged themselves tempted by the banks and lenders by design—the Coachmen.

CHAPTER 4

DIVORCED

It turned out that those two gentlemen who entertained Nadia that night were divorce attorneys who ironically represented Nadia to get her the better end of the divorce deal. At the swing of the Judge's gavel, Nadia received 100% full custody of Summer, alimony, and child support with a restraining order, never allowing Geo to return home again. The court needlessly went hard on Geo, and even though things were tough enough, Geo did not fight. If he fought against Nadia, having a mutual interest in Summer and reflecting on what little financial reserves were currently available, Geo believed more harm would be done in the short-term by fighting her in court instead of strategizing a long-term path forward beyond this turmoil.

Geo chose to evade these setbacks for now.

Geo was used to taking on worldly challenges against him, and he would protect his family and interests to the bitter end. Still, he had never encountered challenges internally from within, as he had recently witnessed with his wife and career. He was conflicted by all that transgressed, but he looked further into the future and saw the larger picture. Nadia was not a bad mother. Nadia just became a terrible disloyal wife and a nasty woman for all of her sinful ways, greed, and womanly reasons, she did what she had to do, and that had nothing to do with Geo. As a mother, at least Nadia took care of Summer, and Geo understood this, and he had very little choice in the matter anyway. Life and destiny took over his timeline as a husband and father, but at least Geo had Nadia as leverage. Things could have been much worse as he put his feelings aside, gathered an emotional skin of leather, and saved what emotional energy he had left.

A man's primal instinct is to survive and find methods to financially support his daughter for his family and their future. It wouldn't have mattered anyway what and how Geo thought of his marriage and his love for Nadia, the market crashed anyway, and his life savings and reliability as a provider would have diminished quickly if he did not do something fast to find a way to bring in more income. Everything was lost for Geo. He had no time to mourn or to be angry at the divorce or Nadia, at the least for the moment, they had a home with a roof over their heads, and of course, Nadia had good legal representation to keep her company at night to Geo's demise. Geo's trust account bled to zero value, and he had minimal cash left, and a career that previously provided him a good income was only as good as the real estate deals, he was closing that day. Zero real estate deals closed during the 2008-2010 market crash. So, Geo thought there must be jobs in a bigger city, so he packed his luggage some cloths and business suits and drove his car to San Francisco.

CHAPTER 5

THE BIG LITTLE CITY

Geo left the suburbs for San Francisco. He called it a *Big Little City.* It is an international city that incorporated every iconic Wall Street corporation and business one could imagine, yet with shorter work weeks than in New York City. Employees would show up to work at 12pm Mondays and leave at 12pm on Fridays. The people in this Big Little City were like the inhabitants of a small rural town, and yet you had the contrast of tall skyscrapers filled with VC and Wall Street firms, the leading social media platforms, and all the tech firms that wet nursed them.

Geo moved into a seedy, rat-infested, bedbug-ridden small hotel located in the old beatnik North Beach District called "Little Italy," which now was a neighborhood of young, optimistic, progressive liberal minded millennials who thrived like bees in a hive as they labored for the tech companies and corporations in the financial district.

North Beach had strip bars, adult venues, restaurants, clubs, and lounges where these millennials would hang out after work, drinking, snorting an inordinate amount of cocaine, and ingesting moly socially. Millennials were the teen spawn outgrowth of Gen Xers, now young adults raised on TV sitcoms like Friends and movies such as The Wolfe of Wall Street. These people were concerned with outward appearances, living lifestyles most could not afford, with egos harvested from the outside rather than from within. They were hand fed and suckled, spoiled rotten by their parents who were bent on fairness and utopian reasoning when their children would win trophies in any sport, even in last place. Millennials had little trust and allegiance to anyone, so they could not be allied with either. They were sold the idea that marijuana was the best next thing since a loaf of sliced white bread. And they projected their half-baked philosophies to their parents, hook, line, and sinker, who approved their many methods of desensitizing themselves with pot and eventually drugs. After all, the California government was behind the push to dumb down this generation using drugs from the governor to legislators to Ivy league and local college campus presidents who promoted the legalized sales of these drugs with fallacious bigoted paid for studies that came out of prestigious leftist progressive doctors and professors who were all tied to the collegiate system.

Geo couldn't stand the sight of a flakey millennial as it opposed every conservative value system he had. Millennials! Young know-it-alls without wisdom, style, or grace; exactly the type of individuals the corporations needed to program with progressive ideologies while they worked. These types of people would not commit to anything; even if they did, their words and promises were useless and unreliable. They would never pay up on a sports bet if they lost. It was a minor observation, although Geo maintained his distance from them, and when he dealt with them, he would have the upper hand. Geo came from a background where a person's word meant his integrity.

Even Elon Musk had his day with these twenty-something misguided seedlings when, via a hostile proxy merger, he purchased Twitter, then fired nearly 80% of them to sever uneconomical, non-working, nonproductive millennial fat that they represented in Twitter's San Francisco headquarters and rebranded Twitters name to "X" as Elon's mark to show opposition and change. At other tech companies, stock prices rose anytime a new management team stepped into any corporation that fired a herd of these toxic millennials if they could. That is how bad they were at work. If they were not taking selfies of themselves to post on FB, they become irrelevant, using nearly 1/3 of the workday on company time chatting on their smartphones. The Millennials became the hatchlings to the "Woke" generation. If Millennials were caterpillar's cocooning, then the Woke Generation were the moths that metamorphosed into a defunct generational gap in America's workforce and productivity. They perfected smartphone texting, dating, and purchasing online goods and feared personal confrontation, making them terrible at communications and salespeople. They couldn't negotiate anything good in a deal. Millennials would not commit to anything; even if they did, their words and promises were useless and unreliable.

CHAPTER 6

GLOBALIST AGENDA

Is it their fault? These millennials are instrumental to the globalist in every way. The globalist had a well-orchestrated propaganda plan for this generation as this generation was the first connected to technology at birth, biometrically, physically, and emotionally, eventually forming their characters and personalities. With the advent of computers, laptops, smartphones, social media platforms, and programmed Hollywood movies, media is digital food for them to mentally eat, swallow, digest, absorb, and grow into programmable robots like no other generation. The globalist rewards them with junk food, brownies and marijuana at their corporate lunch room and café.

The larger smartphone companies had millennials hooked like netted fish catch floundering for life in a container from the original smartphones to each succeeding smartphone and stepping them up gradually from operating system to operating system via updates on their phones, computers, and online platforms. Millennials would line up for weeks awaiting the newest technological update. This was normal for them. They were all up to date in their mental neural wiring, just as planned. Now programmed to the hilt and herded like sheep to believe any propaganda they were given. In fact, every social media platform, website, and corporation tracked these Millennials and formed their thoughts based on their personal data, from posts to comments about what they purchased. The platform algorithms knew them better than they knew themselves. They grew up on digital games since they were children, and their entire lifestyles were formatted within their brains using technological tools. Their minds were captured to control their hearts for their wallets and votes, whatever they were told. They are the most highly malleable generation of any generation in the past. They were programmed, socially pressured, or frightened to do things they most likely would not do naturally as humans if they had never touched a smartphone or computer. The perfect generation to implement globalist agendas and movements.

Geo learned very quickly how the poor lived in San Francisco. The city that seemed so international started to appear to be multifaceted. The city natives gained more character and were more life-like to Geo as he lived among the natives. He started to see the financial caste between the rich, the poor, and the middle class. The natives had to live in close proximity to each other compared to neighbors safely across the lawn in the suburbs. Therefore, they all learned to police each other and how to deal with neighbors a little more patiently, even when someone would blow a mental fuse from time to time. The natives were mostly uninterested in anyone's private business and mostly respectful, although there were high crime rates and addictions in the city, tarnishing all of San Francisco from the Golden Gate and Bay Bridge inward.

It is a sanctuary city, so San Francisco welcomes every illegal immigrant from the world, including ex-convicts just released from prison. This city was a perfect crucible for convicts to harbor themselves, as no questions were asked, unlike in the suburbs, where neighbors are warned about possible pedophiles or convicts moving into the neighborhood. Seemingly it was used as a leftist political ploy for votes allowing every appreciative illegal immigrant and convict to vote liberal and progressively. The politicians and media would have you think otherwise, but this was the unspoken rule when you lived and worked in the city.

The city legislators, politicians, and government employees gave out perks to the sanctuaried convicts in return for their biased favored vote. Lifelong government handouts include affordable housing, government food handouts, government funding, and even a regular menu of drugs, alcohol, and cigarettes free to the addicted. It was almost as if the government was rearing its socialistic tendencies because these handouts were not temporary but were counted on as an everyday mainstay for the afflicted, giving them no motivation to do anything grand in their lives, but to vote in one direction, the direction that kept them getting free governmental handouts forever.

American welfare was supposed to be temporary and as-needed, but not in San Francisco. On the other hand, you had the very wealthy people; most were merely rich as their families became affluent as real estate values increased. Others were trust fund babies of deceased hard-working middle-class parents of the '60s and '70s.

Wealthy people worldwide had iconic corporate businesses in San Francisco that bought properties in affluent neighborhoods like the Marina District and Cow Hollow. San Francisco is a corner of the world when it comes to commerce that attracts wealthy people to live here.

Geo couldn't ruminate much about the middle class, like lawyers, doctors, and small business owners, as the legislation and incentives disfavored them in every way. If they invested their life savings in a business and hired a manager, they would give that employee more rights than the owner in operating any business. If they had invested in real estate, the lower-class people would take over their rental property, and the laws were covertly written to allow them to take part of the homeowner's investment and equity. If the renter did not pay their rent, even though there was subsidized affordable housing, it was an impossible legal fight to evict any tenant. So, the middle class is not incentivized to gain any wealth, especially amid astronomical taxes in any financial dealing or gains.

The socialistic-leaning nonprofit agencies were initially designed for good holistic social causes. Still, they became monstrous real estate investing machines buying out middle-class single and multi-family homeowners to create affordable housing for the poor and to spread Marxist propaganda for the globalist who donates to the fake causes that kept the poor hooked to their agenda and government handouts.

The globalist has an agenda to crush the middle class out of San Francisco so that there would be a very thick line of poor people relying on government handouts and a very narrow line of the wealthy dictating the rules and policies for the poor. This agenda was started in the 1970s and has continued but reared its ugly head as the market crashed in 2008 and is still on the course today as the middle class continues to be phased out by these political and elite controllers.

As Geo analyzed the situation, he realized this was the fundamental building of Marxist socialism in America. In fact, the city leaders, nonprofits, and corporations admitted to it boldly any chance they could. Although Californians were oblivious to this plan, and the millennials, of course, could not give a damn if they were free or under a tyrannical government. Developers were encouraged to build more nonprofit types of affordable housing. The idea was zero ownership of anything for citizens, consistent with socialistic propaganda of "diversity, equity, and inclusion (DIE) which was merely socialism cloaked in fairness created by the United Nations and NGO agendas 2021 and 2030. Everyone in San Francisco was progressive, rich or poor, but they had no clue what it meant, just like *The Stupid Little Boys*.

CHAPTER 7

MILLENNIAL SYNDROME

Geo did not like San Francisco. He thought it was too cold, too foggy, and too muggy. When he had visited in the past, he felt the buildings cast dark shadows everywhere, baring sunlight from getting indoors for most of the day. However, San Francisco appeared to be a moving economy, and plenty of tech jobs were listed on CL chat boards and Job recruiters hunted corporate heads feverishly.

Geo spent hours parked in front of a Coffee Shops using their WIFI on his laptop. He was temporally sleeping in his car and desperately looking for jobs on his computer. Geo set up his first interview with Sea's Candy Corporation, backed by Bricksure Hartherway, for a position as a commercial real estate support assistant to the real estate director. All of the Sea's Candy stores and kiosk contracts were written on hard copy paper and files, and they needed help in digitizing and converting those manual files to PDFs and Excel spreadsheets, a skill Geo believed he could do.

Geo got up early that morning and rushed into the gym, where he took a quick shower before the interview. The gym's hot water was broken, so Geo took a quick cold shower and prepared his partially wrinkled suit for the interview. He looked chumpy, but at least he was in a suit for the interview. He was introduced to HR Director Candy M. Savene, a distressed, plump, overworked middle-aged, divorced single woman with four children who worked at Sea's Candy for over 30 years. As Geo walked in, she sized him up from head to toe as if Geo was in a nightclub for a first date with her. Geo felt from that point on that the interview was lost as she didn't seem friendly at all. Somehow this ratcheted poor, overweight lady with an unflattering oversized crooked boob job must have suffered a life of work and no freedom or some unlikely event with a man because she was asking Geo personal questions as opposed to professional ones, and it appeared as if Geo was getting the brunt of all of Candy's life misgivings. Geo left the failed interview in utter shock.

This, coupled with Geo's over serious demeanor and overconfidence in knowing that he could do this job, conflicted the interview all together. Geo was, in a way, relieved that maybe the job was not suitable for him as he disgracefully returned to his car and his abode for now.

Geo continued interviewing with various companies in San Francisco for two months and was tired of sleeping in his car. The tech companies and recruiting agencies sought programming skills rather than sales skills from former real estate agents. Geo found his plan more complicated than expected as his cash flow dwindled by the day. Geo was becoming desperate. Companies were seeking the quintessential millennial employee as, for some reason, anyone over 40 was considered over the hill as an employee in San Francisco.

Night and day, Geo was emailing resumes and filling employment applications in his car parked in front of a Starbucks. He ran out of change and stopped paying the parking meters, and before he knew it, he had a stack of parking tickets that grew. The city's parking enforcement specialist were relentless, and the parking tickets were over hundred dollars each. Every parking spot in the city came with a cursed parking meter. One day as he ran into the gym to take a quick shower, he returned to his car, and the front wheel had a boot attached to the tire. Geo had to chalk over $2,000 in unpaid parking tickets that he didn't have. So, Geo was left with a suitcase in his hand when his car was towed away. On foot now in the rain, Geo still had some survival money tucked away, but it was quickly running out. He found and rented per month what was called an SRO.

One night as Geo was reformatting his resume, he gazed

up and saw a bug peering at him from the wall in his dimly lit Edwardian-styled single-room occupancy (SRO) hotel room, meaning affordable city-subsidized hotel for the sanctuaried poor that had inches old of caked interior smoke tarnished paint on to the walls and a subtle foul smell of old wet, rotted wood intermixed with the smell of an old yellowish worn sluggish shag rug placed in the room. He quickly shot his wide-open hand to the wall to slap the bug flat dead, and when the bug splattered, it squirted a puddle of thick blood onto the wall that it had sucked from Geo's ankles the night before. Geo learned the meaning of bed bugs at that very moment. Every soul that slept in that SRO complex had bedbugs biting them left and right. The city called these hotels SRO's, which were used to house wayfarers, ex-convicts, illegal immigrants, drug addicts, and prostitutes who had little money and could not afford an average hotel. But the city government over-billed these hotel rooms for their subsidized clients. There was a drug dealer that controlled every floor. At the least, Geo had a roof over his head at the moment and a mattress where he could at least get some sleep.

One late evening Geo could not concentrate on his laptop and work in finding employment because he was tired of hearing the regular brutal beating of an abusing drunken, six-foot hardened black man beating on his meth-addicted white tattooed gender dysphoric girlfriend every night. In the daytime, he could hear them fucking the morning away like nothing ever happened. The yells and cries of the "lady" were loud but with a manly tone, and no one could help. It was as if Geo had been brought back to a time when there was no civility. There is no technology generation or time passage in a ghetto. A ghetto is always a never changing ghetto no matter how much time passes.

San Francisco had its share of ghettos in every district in one form or another due to its socialistic tendencies, even in the wealthy neighborhoods. No one dared call the police as the "lady" would not press charges anyway. The police hands were tied as the city district attorney would not press charges, and the person would be released that same day to cause more trouble without bail. Apparently, the district attorney (DA) received donations for his election as San Francisco's DA from globalists and Hugo Chavez, his old employer Venezuela's communist president and left-is socialist step-parents who were once on the FBI's most wanted list as terrorists, so consequently, the justice system was leaning towards socialism as well. This is how these people lived and negotiated their terms of subsidized living. It was their way of not working and finding every way of getting perpetually diluted with drugs and alcohol and high and having fun at the government's expense, even it if meant a nightly beating. Geo withered every domestic issue within that SRO as there was never a justified remedy worth sacrificing any time or sleep. There was a perpetual cycle of misfits always circulating each room of that SRO which gave much reason for Geo to find employment urgently before he lost his bitter mind and accepted the terms of the ghetto all together.

CHAPTER 8

LIPO LOUNGE DRAGON LADY

It is mid-February during Chinese New Year, and Chinatown is celebrating with Longwu, dragon dancers and fireworks on the semi foggy streets and tight corridors and alleys. Geo found himself in North Beach, washing away his sorrows with alcohol at Devils Acre bar. Hearing the fireworks blocks away in Chinatown, Geo started walking there. He passed the Lipo Lounge on Grant Street and stopped for a drink. As Geo orders a Chinese Mai Tai, a mysterious traditionally dressed Asian lady sitting next to him at the bar is flirting. The bartender calls her Dragon Lady as he hands her a Mai Tai as well. Geo senses something out of kilter and insidious about her. Geo lingers to not be impolite, yet finishes the drink and leaves to escape the Dragons Lady's seduction. Suddenly, as he exits the door threshold everything outside is blurry, and Geo feels faint. Out of nowhere and in the midst of people, fireworks and new year festivity commotion, Geo is dragged into an alley by three thugs of the Triad gang. As fireworks blare overhead, Geo is beaten, repeatedly kicked in the head, robbed, and left for dead.

Geo awakens from a lucid comatic dream of his daughter Summer and him connecting the zodiac constellations on Yucatan beach. As he re-awakens in the midst of the interior of a martial arts studio to the thoughtful gaze of Sensei Li Mi Chen. Li Mi Chen found Geo in the flooded alley, took him home, and treated his wounds. Geo, very weak and unable to speak, falls into a coma once again. As days pass, Geo is healing. Li observes Geo is struggling and decides to take him under his wing. He offers Geo training in the ancient wisdom of martial arts.

A spiritual man with a killer instinct, Li is humbly wealthy and has a collection of modern weaponry. As Geo healed each day, he witnessed martial arts students training with Li in the art of Win Chung. Although it was more than mere training, they were preparing. Li had more insight as time soon revealed.

Yue Chen, Li's daughter awakens Geo with hot tea. She is a meek, traditional servant of the Win Chung order, and yet she is a martial arts warrior. Yue questions Geo who he is and why he was beaten. Geo looks at her and explains, "I was mugged by the Triads Gang of Chinatown apparently, remnants of the Raymond Shrimp-Boy Clan. And it appears I'm having a hard time in life right now." As he replied ironically.

In the background, Win Chung trainers practice on wooden dummy poles, and Geo asks where Li is. Yue says, "You are in good hands and will remain here until you are fully healed. As she turns to leave, she trips on a bamboo mat, and the porcelain tea cup falls from her tray. Geo reaches with lightning speed to catch the tea cup before it hits the ground. Yue exclaims, "Wow, you're fast." Geo says, "I used to work as a grocery store bagger. Fast reflexes catching all those cans thrown at me." She smiles at his modesty.

Li Mi Chen's Win Chung Order trained for many years since their separation from the Hong Kong Order. And the same Order in which famous martial artist trained on Commercial Street in Chinatown. After the murder of San Francisco's Chinese Mayor, the decay of civility in San Francisco proliferated. The Chinese Mayor was a dear friend of Li Mi Chen of the same ancestral family.

Right before he was murdered, The Mayor warned Li Mi Chen of an upcoming event that would be catastrophic to the public. The news reported The Chinese Mayor died of a heart attack at age 65. Yet, in fact, he was poisoned in a San Francisco supermarket with a shellfish toxin firearm developed by the CIA in the 1970s, which caused nervous system failure and heart attacks with no trace of the poison via a gun dart. The mayor's suspicious death ushered in a new female black bisexual socialist leaning mayor, who was part of a larger sinister group as her boyfriend a city supervisor was currently being incarcerated for a multi-million-dollar fraud case. Li Mi Chen was fully aware of the reason for the assassination and things to come.

The times were closing in, and many mysterious groups in San Francisco were secretly virtue signaling to each other and the public that change was about to occur in plain sight with iconic references in different forms. The high-rise building's lights were all changed to Venetian purple, and the Trans America light was changed from white to purple. Li Mi Chen saw these trends and sought new warriors to train for his Win Chung order, but he held on to this secret.

One late evening Geo finally gets the energy to stand and walk from the patio to the dojo as his training has improved his strength day at a time. He comes to the geniqua wooden target dummy post and mimics the Win Chung movements. Li Mi Chen walks into the dojo, pairs up on another post, and leads Geo. As they continue, Geo confesses to Li Mi Chen that things are somehow not right within himself and the world. Geo stops and ask, "I don't know what is wrong, but I sense things are not quite right. Everything I know and see is upside down, and I have nothing left." Li Mi Chen remains silent. Night after night, Geo gets up and practices the movements. Li Mi Chen, without words, begins to train him. They both know they are on the same frequency. They both see and feel the heavy air and intrinsically know they are preparing for something big. There is a shooting range below the dojo, so as Geo becomes traditionally trained in Win Chung, he also trains with combat guns, spears, knives, and sticks. Months pass. Geo feels in more physical control of himself and his destiny. Inspired by Li Mi Chen, he became the standard of sound ethics and spirituality in Geo's life.

CHAPTER 9

COMMISSIONED

Geo is low on funds and continues to seek employment. The mortgage industry is in disarray, so his skill set is obsolete, at least for now. His recruiter Edwin, tells him about a small notary public opportunity that works with Geo's schedule. So, Geo registers with the Secretary of State, passes the Notary exam, and gets his commission and his ink stamp.

Geo assessed the market, and very few notaries in the financial district (Fidi) near Chinatown are accessible to the public regularly. On his first day, Geo is assigned a mobile notarization appointment in an older building in the Fidi. As he enters the elevator, the building décor is dated and eerie; the secretary is young, although she does not make eye contact with Geo. Her dress style is plain, unmemorable and neutral, like the rest of her face. Geo states that he is there to notarize Mr. Lawrence Silverstern. With approval, she leads Geo down a long stark hallway to an office where a 70ish balding hotel executive wearing a purple tie and dark blue suit sits behind his heavy wooden desk. The furniture is antiquated but clean and well-maintained. Like time has stopped. Mr. Silverstern asks his secretary to leave and pushes the documents to be notarized before Geo. The document paper feels oddly thick As Geo gets to work, Silverstein hovers over his shoulder. Geo realizes that Silverstein owns many of the hotels in the city. All of their insurance policies are being renewed and those require notarizations.

Geo looks around the antiquated office and recognizes different iconic shapes within statutes and artwork while signing and stamping the thick documents for several hours. Geo notices the people in the photos look odd but doesn't give it much thought. As Geo finishes the job, Mr. Silverstern hands him a substantial check for the numerous notarizations and says, "I will recommend your services; well done." Geo responds, "Thank you, Sir." He was elated that he got the job done well that day. Larry was a but suspicious, mysterious and wonky Geo thought to himself, but at the least he got some income for his work.

It was Geo's first glimpse of his new role as a notary public. Geo didn't think much about anything at this point, but everything that day was recorded in his subconscious. I am a Notary Public Geo whispered out loud. He put the emphasis on public, trying to get a grip on what his new job meant to him. It turned out that doing mobile services paid off as the clients loved the convenience, confidentiality, secrecy and privacy of signing at their immediate location.

On his second assignment, he notarized a gentleman in an older condo complex nested on the side of a hill in the old Russian Hill District of San Francisco. The gentlemen came to his front door masked and wished to be notarized outside the front door. A "Seraph" epidemic was laying siege to the city at this point, and Mr. Degetty did not want to allow anyone into his home due to the virus. Mr. Degetty handed Geo a face mask to put on. Geo smiled respectfully at Mr. Degetty and wore the mask. Geo asked for his ID, placing the thick papered document on a brick wall ledge on his front porch to sign. The header read, "Contact Tracing Agreement New York City Health Department" With no questions, Geo properly identified Mr. DeGetty, and signed and stamped the thick document.

Mr. Degetty said, "We want to make sure that anyone infected is properly secured and treated, and I'll be the one tracking and contacting people for quarantine for everyone's "safety and overall good" Geo noticed that Mr. Degetty wore a purple sweater with a gold pendant in the same iconic triangle within a triangle icon that he saw in Mr. Silverstern's office. Geo observed that Mr. Degetty seemed ready and zealous to control people more than help them. Geo collected his payment and left. Looking back at the house, he thought how odd these people all appeared, not to mention the unique thick bounded paper and unusual thick viscous, embossed ink that the documents were composed of.

So, appointment after appointment, Geo encountered odd, wonky wealthy, and upper middle-higher class individuals all signing documents that were all related in one way or form to affect a larger suspicious action or event. There were either government or non-profit organizations and individuals trying to protect themselves legally from something. Geo noticed peculiarities in the documents. Some ordered military-grade fencing, ovens, industrial building materials, etc. Curiously, all of these individuals had something suspect about them. They all wore purple emblems and had iconic necklaces, statues, lighting, or art on their walls. From appointment-to-appointment Geo started to notice minor but significant details. Multi-million-dollar contracts were being notarized from corporation to corporation, person to person. As he performed more notarizations, Geo was trusted within the in-crowd, going into multi-million-dollar mansions for signings. Geo's reputation and income started to grow. Geo had no secret to his success; he never took note of people's business or the contents of what he was notarizing and was always faithfully prompt to every appointment. The job was not difficult and highly oversimplified. He reminded himself that ignorance is bliss, and the notarial job was easier not knowing anyone's personal or private business but merely getting paid.

Who would imagine a notary public would make a sizable income? But his name and reputation as someone that could keep confidentiality was evolving and imperative to his clientele. So, they paid handsomely for private signing appointments, usually after hours, so Geo's premium fees were more than the monetary value for each notarization. After all, no one could know the secret transactions of all these secretive people and their dubious plans. Geo had no incentive to pre-read any confidential document but merely to notarize the signatures. To identify and witness people signing to the confidentially of what they agreed to was Geo's only priority, not the content.

But as time passed, document after document, Geo could not help to think about what was happening. Strange people and locations and the nervous secretive uneasy atmosphere that came with each individual in signing after signing. Everything that he notarized, every document, had some sinister undertone. The clientele was becoming creepier as time progressed. If it is a trust, a will, a contract, a payment, an agreement, a work order, an affidavit, or an acknowledgment, there always has something sinister about it. All of the documents always came in high-quality heavy-bonded thick paper. Geo thought the paper was handmade, each page thick and lux. Each document's printed font and ink quality came from a special printing process, and the ink was thick as blood. Geo could feel the valleys of each font created in between each letter. Every document either had an embossed hidden insignia that could be felt when Geo gently ran his hand across the paper. All stationary was crafted uniquely.

In some of the signings for particular clients, Geo noticed non-profit organizations being funded by multi-million-dollar donations by large corporations. He saw signed and stamped sizable private payments from foreign governments to district attorneys and politicians within the city. His clientele had something physically unappealing, dark, and shady about them.

Geo couldn't help his curiosity and started to research each individual client after each signing. Although it was out of his job requirement spectrum as a notary public, he could not help but research the lives behind their signatures. Geo rolled out a large city map on his wall and started placing pins on locations, signings, events, people, places, and connections, like stars of constellations. He was looking for trends and answers. He didn't know what he was seeking, but he knew that something sinister was lurking in all of these people and the information he was gathering.

Things start moving faster for Geo. The more information that he gathered, the more inquisitive he became. Geo was referred to Crypto Alley, off Pacific and Montgomery Street in Jackson Square, where all the venture capitalist and ICO platforms were evolving. He signed with every platform, from AngelHiss to Venture Capital to Revere and other major cryptocurrency companies. Node was a local creator shared space hangout and coffee bar where Geo regularly awaited his next assignment. Node was a social geek-tech beehive or rather a hornet's nest of crypto programmers, many with a hacking past and private online security histories. They all gathered there and exchanged ideas and information. CBDC's, digital currency, artificial intelligence (AI) and how governments were moving into a cloud world of exchange, making it easy to control people, their money, behaviors, habits, and survival from the moment they are born and into their grave. These were the topics at geek gatherings and hackathon at Node as some Geo noticed some familiar faces that also trained with Li there.

Geo saw the trends from every direction, and in the interim, he figured out which crypto companies and currencies were succeeding and which were not and which to bet on and invest. Gradually his notary gains became crypto investments to crypto gains. Document after document, notary after notary, client after client, Geo figured out what was trading, trending, and what was not. His crypto investment purchases went from $.000010 per token to $100 to $30,000 per token. He bought thousands of tokens, and he became wealthy in a short time. But Geo did not trust anyone, so he parked every token in private digital wallets and only used and cashed tokens for his daily usage. He purchased gold any chance he could get and stored it in many different locations. But without his key notary public position, the valuable information would cease, and the lucrative and sinister knowledge of what everyone was collaborating on would have no answers and beg no questions.

So as meager paying as the Notary Public Commission seemingly was, he was in a position where data, information, and people were all pivotal in his success. Who, what, where, and when was on his daily agenda, learning what certain people were conspiring. So, Geo continued, secretively on his agenda. He was hungry for the truth while lining his pockets with crypto and converting to gold. It was not greed that trigged Geo, but to overcome the financial breakdowns he suffered in a mere quest for economic survival and independence for all the things that truly mattered in his life. His daughter, Summer and Furthermore, Geo wasn't hurting anyone or stealing anything directly physical from anyone, but merely knowledge.

Geo was creating an arsenal of cash, tokens and gold on instinct that he would need to protect himself from the desperate acts, sign-offs, and treachery looming in his immediate sphere and these seemingly wicked people. Iconography, colors, and symbology in those very thick documents secured everyone's hierarchical status in a complex structure and agenda. All the players in this game were very different, representing themselves, their family lineage, and their intentions. For some reason, they all would vet Geo with trust, as if he had a bloodline to be proud of.

What were all these covert individuals, corporations, non-profits, politicians, and secret societies collaborating to do? What was the grand master agenda? Meanwhile, on the other side of town, some of Geo's clients gather at the Boho Club, a secret society club of grand proportions. Here, politicians and corporate executives gather from around the world to plan and pave the way for our collective future despite the interests of the greater public sentiment.

Many discreet injustices have occurred at this social club, yet all eyes are shut, covered up just like the secret society it is. When these elitist men and their wives gather in separate rooms to stir their drinks with demons of satanic rituals, greed and fame cloud their sight. They give in to evil.

CHAPTER 10

MINA THE DANCER

Across the backyard of the Boho Club, two large wooden doors conceal 24-hour armed security personnel and surveillance cameras facing across Taylor Street into an unassuming basement massage parlor that explicitly services Boho Club members. Geo is called to The Golden Pearl to notarize criminal legal documents for a deaf Asian prostitute named Mina. She is 25, German-Korean, very fit with fake firm breasts, milky white skin, and stunning green eyes that lack life. Unable to hear Geo during their fractured conversation, she claimed she was once Silicon Valley wealthiest tech giant, Lawrence Allison's, lover and had the videos to prove her claim. It turns out that many of the Boho members sneak out of the Club's guarded back doors and cross the street to receive sensual Asian massages at The Golden Pearl regularly.

Although Geo could barely understand Mina's sharp Korean accent, numbed by her deafness, she managed to communicate with body motions. One of the Club members, William Smith, aka Nara, who dated the new bisexual black socialist mayor of San Francisco in the past and was head of San Francisco public governmental agencies, a regarded wealthy member of the club, was one of her regulars before his arrest. Still, after each sexual rendezvous, Nara started manhandling Mina, putting his hand to her face one too many times and leaving her with a black eye and bruised body. Mina could no longer take the abuse. Mina contacted the local police department to file a report.

Ironically, The Boho Club ombudsman became aware of the incident and intercepted the investigation. He knew all of the right people at the precinct and caused the incident to go away. Mina's criminal complaint would disappear into the ether.

And in seeking safety, it becomes Mina's worst nightmare.

Mina was set up by the Boho Club hierarchy, falsely charged with drug procession, arrested and released on bond back to the Golden Pearl brothel. The Madam of the brothel was paid to keep her drugged and would fill her drinks with drugs to sedate Mina daily. Mina was not allowed to say anything about the abuse she encountered. She was threatened. She was in fear for her life. The Madam contacted Geo for his notary services to have Mina sign NDA affidavits to shut Mina up.

When Geo arrived, he was unaware of the situation he was about to engage. He noticed the front door heavily secured behind wrought iron grates along with surveillance cameras. Geo would never imagine this place for a brothel. It was nondescript and conveniently located across the street from the Boho Club to serve its patrons as a regular sex stop for its members.

When Geo rang the doorbell, an older Asian lady appeared to answer the door and led Geo inside. The pungent smell of an old Victorian-styled living room, mixed with the smell of bleach, awakened his senses. Geo saw several young Asian women pass down the hallway dressed in heels and lingerie. The older Asian lady was indeed a Madam.

The Madam had Geo sit on a tuft red leather sofa as she ordered two young Asian prostitutes to bring the faint Mina to the living room. The two young girls held Mina by the arms and assisted her to the couch. Although Mina looked pale and withdrawn, she understood what she needed to do. As a notary public, Geo could not get into personal details with his clients, although he asked her if she understood the document. She nodded and signed the document, which Geo Notarized and later delivered to the courier.

Geo noticed complex brilliant-colored tattoos of snakes, spiders, and owls mixed with circles, squares, and triangle shapes on Mina's body--typical iconography of the Boho Club members and the same for Geo's wonky list of clients. She also had burns on her arm used in their candle rituals and triangle burn scars on her upper chest. While she was signing under the watch of her Madam, Mina slipped Geo a small envelope beneath the papers.

Later that day, walking back to the Dojo where Geo now rented the basement studio from Li Mi Chen, he read Mina's note, and it said they were planning on killing her and had devastating plans for the local people of San Francisco. She would overhear them talk about their plans; The Agenda. She wanted Geo to come back as a "John" so that she could have more time to explain to him.

CHAPTER 11

LIONS DEN

Geo goes back out and lands at "Lion's Den," a bar in the old brothel district in Chinatown. It's another rainy afternoon. Geo orders an old fashion whisky to temporarily desensitize him from everything. The Media shows the Black Lives Marxist (BLM) march and the burning and looting of stores on the flatscreen tv braced on the wall. Some of the patrons are gathered around, watching the scene unfold as the news claims George Floyd overdosed of a fentanyl addiction and yet the fake media changed the narrative to one of racism to contrive division amongst Americans once again.

Geo reflects that women like Mina will never get a fair chance. Slowly he is trying to put all of the pieces of the puzzle together in his mind as the media streams propaganda cloaked as news on the flatscreen. The media is in a frenzy, and with the advent of the Seraph epidemic, congress is asking to take more federal loans. So far, according to the news, the world's national debt is at 225 trillion to world banks, and the rush to find a vaccine. Geo reflects on his map and all of the odd seditious people he signed as a notary public. He realized that the news was merely nothing but a consistent stream of socialist leaning propaganda. The background music to this tale shows more BLM protesting, and at the end story, a video of Russia burning down a tower of babble as the "Breaking News" flash announces the US, UN and NATO support of Ukraine as Ukraine's prime minister "Vladimir Zelensky is shown dancing nude in women's stilettos on the news reel. Somehow an actor with no military experience became a Ukraine's chief in command in full war mode, begging for money to heist from American tax payer's pockets with permission from corrupt American politicians in congress.

Geo turns and sees his friend and attorney he met earlier

that year, a Harvard graduate with an MBA, named Steven James Bradlie, whom Geo affectionally refers to as James, flirting with the Asian host named V at the door of the Lion's Den lounge. Geo orders a second round for both of them, as both greet each other when James approaches Geo's cocktail table. "Long time no see Geo," James says, "You look good. You been working out? I got your text exclaims James. What's going on?" Geo exclaims, "Maybe you can tell me?" James, with a blind look, says, "Touché." So, Geo pushes the whiskey over to James and starts to explain to James about Mina and that he didn't know what to do about her and the entire scandalous scenario.

Geo further goes into great detail and tells James that he believes something of a grand conspiracy is going on in San Francisco, which will reflect with the world as well, between the wealthy people, certain secret societies, groups, and politicians, and that the police won't adequately respond to Mina's murder plot and her note. They all seem to be planning something significant and detrimental to the public, but Geo doesn't know what it is.

Although when Geo tries to explain to James what he discovered through his notarial meetings and his theories and analysis, Geo brings up the name of William Smith Nara, the person who he thinks murdered Mina, and as soon as Geo utters Nara's name, James aggressively tries to silence Geo. James loudly tells Geo, "Shut Up," James continues, "Do you know exactly what you're dealing with here?" What are you some kind of conspiracy theorist now?" Don't you know who Nara is? He is the head of one of San Francisco's main governmental agencies. Nara is listed in the World Economic Forum and donates heavily to many nonprofit organizations and politicians here and in the world governments. Do not say things like that, or you will lose your business, and all these people will defiantly shut you out. I am giving you sound advice, Geo, as your friend and attorney. Listen to me!"

At that moment, Geo realizes that his lawyer, James, although not tainted by corruption, is spiritually blinded by complacency and lacks a spine. Afraid to be uncool, he is cavalier, afraid of sticking out like a sore thumb and against his liberal-minded friends. Geo realizes at that point that James is soft in the middle and completely spineless. Geo responds to James "You blind son of a bitch, you see everything wrong happening here and now, and you don't say a thing! Our cities are being destroyed, looting, a drug overdose epidemic, muggings, and robbing. The girl at the café just got pistol whipped and robbed. Watch the fucking news; it is all there in front of your eyes! California's assembly members passed a law allowing abortions 28 days after a child's birth. It's a murderous baby body part business racket! Can't you see the world is coming undone right before you? You have your fucking Seraph mask on tighter than a fucking man thong, and you don't question authority? You look ridiculous with that mask on, man!! And yet you cannot see a damn thing. You're blinded by choice! You are blinded by complacency! You're a mad, programmed man, James!

You know, James, in the 1930s, Hitler whispered in the Jews' ears for 20 years that he was going to annihilate them, and at first, none of them would believe his threats because they were doing well in life and in business in Germany and didn't want to ruin their complacent lifestyles. But then Hitler's crew started to take things away through attrition as Hitler gained power. First, he took over the media and gave the Jews socialist crafted propaganda. Then they couldn't gather together in groups or even worship their God. The SS had to stand 6 feet from them so that they would not catch any viruses from the Jews, and little by little, Hitler's Brown Shirt posse took everything away, and at that point, Jews started to listen, but it was too damn fucking late. They were already standing in line at the gas chambers James!

Like now, some Jews were so in denial that they thought they were taking a shower. They ended up in mass graves. Wake up, man! Doesn't this all sound too familiar? We are in the same fucking boat now, and history is repeating itself in a bad way.

Are you blind, man? Do you think death would come looking any different? How far does all of this have to go before you wake up, man? Here I am, your friend in trust, yet you cannot trust what I am trying to tell you, James? I cannot believe you're an attorney. You took an oath to uphold the US Constitution, and even with the media censoring free speech, you say nothing. You have become an enigma, James!" I cannot believe my own friend is trying to silence me because of his own fears now. You are a coward man!

Geo continues his declaration, "James let me read you a quote from Hermann Goering, one of Hitler's chief engineers, on how to conquer and kill the Jews. Maybe this will awaken you? Geo pulls out his phone and reads, "It was very easy. It has nothing to do with Nazism. It has something to do with human nature. You can do it in a Nazi, a socialist, a communist regime, a monarchy, and even in a democracy. The only thing that needs to be done to enslave people is to scare them. If you scare people, you can make them do what you want."

So along with being complacent, you are scared, too, right? The media and peer pressure make you scared until you cannot see clearly, right?" They got you by the ball's son."

Maybe it was the whisky, but Geo felt compelled to tell James how he really felt. Geo had lived a long enough life to live with no regrets. In no way was Geo going to let himself down.

At this point, James is unwilling to listen, and no matter how many times Geo tries to convince him, Geo realizes that his friend James has never changed anything about himself since he met him months ago at the Battery Social Club. Geo remembers some of James's past girlfriends would call him spineless, and for the past 15 years, he owned the same car, furniture, everything. When they went to bars, James had the same routine and clothing style, and now it all made sense to Geo. Geo realized that James was happy and complacent surviving in that manner, even though the Seraph epidemic was defining new life, death and meaning for people, let alone the conspiracy building up. James would never change, let alone save himself from a sinking ship, and at that epiphany, Geo let him go as a friend emotionally. In fact, Geo feared him now. Geo feared that someone so close could not and did not want to see reality as it unfolded, which threatened Geo. In a last sign and gesture of defeat, Geo ordered two shots of Hibiki whiskey, saluted his friend, "To Owls and Spiders and Snakes," stood up from the cocktail table and left his friend at the lounge.

As Geo walked out of the bar, James saluted Geo and yelled, "Are you talking to yourself, Geo? Welcome to the Land of The Free! Geo replied, so as long as I have my 1st amendment next to me it doesn't matter what I yell now does it James? And I don't give a flying fuck if it offends you or your lefty friends, James! Last I heard hate speech is part of my 1st amendment right, so deal with being offended as it beats any gas chamber and tyrannical socialist government and yet you still don't wake up, but when you do, I'll have my 2nd Amendment waiting to protect my 1st amendment. Come to think of it, I don't recall ever seeing a law book in your Condo or office you failed Ivy league attorney! Geo doesn't mean to be rude, although James's ignorance of facts and unwillingness to trust Geo is mind boggling to him.

CHAPTER 12

GEO'S DECLARATION

Geo turns around and walks back into the bar to tell James and everyone there listening, one last old story about a lobster. "James, every time, right before a lobster sheds its crustacea's shell to grow, it suffers great discomfort as it has a soft internal body sustained by its hard exoskeleton. The soft tissue of the lobster rubs and presses against the hard skeleton, causing pain and discomfort to the lobster, which indicates to the lobster that it is time to shed and lose its shell! If it didn't shed its shell, the lobster's natural physical instinct to grow will create so much pressure within its internal body that its internal organs would burst, and the lobster would die. Sometimes, James, we must be willing to grow and get out of our comfort zone, no matter how much discomfort or pain we feel. To complicate things, life and society sometimes force us to grow out of mental and emotional shells for our own health and even physical safety. But Americans and the world population have become oblivious to whether the pressure comes from internal or external influences. They can't tell the difference between growing as a person under their control or someone else's, which may have detrimental consequences for their health and life. It seems to me, James, that everyone has become Comfortable Complicit, Compliant, and Complacent.

The 4 C's, I call it. No, not of credit as in the real estate and lending industries, but the 4 Cs of Change. No one reads or researches history, but history has always been paved not only through hard work and sweat but often through bloodshed and wars. The New York Times estimates of the past 3,400 years, humans have been entirely at peace for 268 of them or just 8 percent of recorded history. The truth is other countries are at war at this very minute, and the death rate continues to grow in staggering numbers. A conveyor belt of bloody dead bodies and souls every minute, day, and year. It is as if war was designed and created to sacrifice humans to evil Gods. How many people have died at war?

At least 108 million people were killed in wars in the twentieth century. Estimates for the total number killed in wars throughout human history range from 150 million to 1 billion. Do you know what a billion is, James? If you killed two million people per year in war for the next approximate 500 years, then that would add up to a billion James. If you can feel anything, imagine that. Imagine one dead body in your posh condominium James! Now is it hitting home?

Sadly, the victors of war make up and create fake history, always favoring their agendas and their religions, and vastly apart from the truth. And the victors and their conspirators always profit from these wars.

Speaking of conspirators and profiteer of war, did you know that one of our recent president's fathers, was a conspirator and aligned his corporations with the Nazis in the 1930s? His father went against the Trading with Enemies Act trading in various forms with Hitler. His company assets were ceased by the American government in 1942 for his part in working with Hitler, ironically his grandson, a succeeding US president put us into a war in the middle east that was incited by the Globalist Zionist inside attack at the Twin Towers and then blamed it on Bin Ladin. Declassified documents today show that even after The United States got sucked into WW2 and when there was already significant information about the Nazis' plans and projections, He worked for and profited from companies closely involved with the German businesses that financed Hitler's rise to power. It has also been suggested that the money he made from these dealings helped to establish the His family fortune and set up its political dynasty. So why do we trust these same corporations that house, feed, and provide for our livelihood supply chains to exist as a society and never question them? The pharmaceutical companies are in a constant state of lawsuits for what can be up to more than 10 billion dollars in total laws suits from medical injuries caused by their medications, including drugs such as many drugs approved by the FDA. Imagine them trying to create a vaccine to cure any upcoming viruses. Do you even read James? Or you just plop your lazy fat ass in front of the TV set every evening after work to see what the contrived fake news provided by the fake media empires owned by six global media news outlets spewing the same programmed news ½ hour at a time breakfast lunch and dinner?

People are too comfortable, James, to understand that maybe history is repeating itself. The millennials sit around drinking alcohol, diluting themselves with drugs or video games, technology, selfies, porn, sex, and distractions, while the older generations are tuned in to movies, fake news, sports, video games and physically unhealthy lifestyles drinking wine every evening, affording every worldly pleasure to brag about over a glass of wine in some fancy high-end anti-bourgeoisie restaurant or establishment.

Everyone is complicit. Taking orders so easily from authorities. Because they ignore the bloody side of history, they trust anyone they perceive in their complicity to be authoritative, especially when frightened into complicity as we are seeing now with the seraph virus.

People comply with the laws, guidelines, and regulations without order. Especially when they are scared to death! They are programmed with soft spots and emotional strings in their hearts, and for anything related to safety and health. They are mentally programmed to be emotional and cave into these orders even if they are being lied to. They are programmed with triggers to melt down and comply when necessary. They trust illicit collegiate studies from Ivy league colleges, they trust science, they trust fake history, they trust corrupt politicians, the fake news, they trust it all, James without question. But they don't trust common sense. They don't trust the common folk and mainly distrust their family and neighbors more, affecting their stability, security, and comfort.

You don't even trust me, James! Just admit it damn it!! You are a fool and will perish just like all the others in history, James. You must be thinking I am a nut case by now. But that is your fallacy! Your mistake, and that, my friend, is what makes you a complete douche bag! The worst part is that you have become a douche bag just like all the other people here that try to convince me that being Comfortable, Complicit, Compliant, and Complacent is the most secure way for me to handle my life and situations like this and to obey those written laws and if I do not comply you try to censor me and shut me up as you did try today, James.

This is one of the reasons why history always repeats in bloodshed. Not merely because there are evil people and evil agendas for evil reasons out there, James but because of this innate flaw that humans are programmed within them and because they are too afraid to get out of their lobster shells and comfort zones. James. You can see it as a flaw or a blanket of security, but it yields the same result in the end. Just ask the 1940's Jews, dead or alive. They will tell you the truth because the living ones survived it and saved themselves and the others didn't listen.

Is it possible that we are all programmed like bees in a beehive only to see the chores of harvesting honey, oblivious to what actually happens in reality? Are we in a matrix? Are we built in with filtered brains, and is our vision blocked or filtered not to see reality, and yet we are so arrogant to think that we are intelligent, individual and free? We do things so subconsciously that I am starting to think that there is something more out there to life based on what I am gathering today, James.

How do hypnotists hypnotize the unconscious side of people? Are we all hypnotized, James? Did someone or something make us this way and purposely program our subconscious to see things or not see things on cue? Did Darwin's evolution just create this programmable side as a security switch in us for our own security and safety, keeping us in the beehive and in a box where by looking outside fears us and we stay inside the box for our own safety, never pushing any boundaries that are to question creating a cyclical programming within us.

You are an arrogant man, James! And a douche bag now to me! You are a fool, and now you scare and threaten me just by your very existence because you represent a break in the chain link of my security. How can I ever trust anyone too comfortable in their own lives when death and destruction are whispering to them, just like Hitler whispered to the Jewish ears 20 years before his henchmen assassinated 12 million Jewish. There were a few smart Jews that left after they gave one warning to their families about what was to become of Nazi Germany. How could they not listen when his propaganda machine was set to full-swing mode every day of those 20 years. Little by little, through a process of attrition, Hitler tore the Jews apart from society and themselves. Some of the Jews even denied the fact that they were being killed. Instead, they took showers of Zyklon B, cyanide, or carbon monoxide exhaust gases. They blindly walked into the gas chambers.

Oh, by the way, Lenin and Marx also gave the Romanovs 20 years of warning and battle before Russia became Marxist, socialist, and communist in 1917-1919, and then 1-2 years later, China became the same, followed by parts of European countries such as Portugal and Spain, with 70 other countries to follow. Each and every time a country flipped to socialism, there was a great famine in each of those countries it seems. Why do you think they all share that fucked up-looking, angry, clenched fist as an icon of their arrival and power stay? They are all the same! They were all given adequate warning. evil always announces its arrival and it has arrived again today.

I believe evil, as a rule, will always announce itself before it sets in. To me, it appears like an unwritten spiritual law that must be adhered to before any bad thing happens to anyone on this earth, individually or as a society; one merely has the power to be still and listen to the echo of things. You, James, and

Everyone are not listing, comfortable, complicit, compliant, and complacent.

Shame on you!! It fears me that you do not listen, and you created such a weak link and a security breach in my life. I cannot trust you now. I would be afraid to be around you, James. Goodbye my good friend. I only roll with lions and titans.

Geo left and didn't look back. He believed James had no clue, still oblivious after all the rhetoric he spewed, it was just another whiskey meetup for James, a drunken spatter, but Geo was determined it was their last meet as trusted friends. Geo knew that was the last time he would ever communicate with his new ex-friend Mr. Steven James Bradlie. Geo realized at that point that he only wanted people he could trust around him. He realized that most of his friends amounted to nothing but a large party at his expense. Geo was determined to expose what he discovered to the world, whether his friends would believe him or not. He was disappointed at his new revelations about his friends. But now he feared them as well. A firm emotional boundary manifested within him at that moment. Geo's social network of friends would shrink over time and he would be more selective about whom he would trust within his life and circle.

Geo receives return calls from the local newspaper editor and the local news channel, who tells him they don't print conspiracy theories, when Geo reached out to them with his findings. So, Geo creates a social media account to tell the world to break the conspiracy agenda in San Francisco, but everyone turned on him when he broke and posted the story. The opinion driven fact-checkers shut his account down due to violating community guideline standards. His Conspiracy theories did not reflect current programmed norms, and they reported him to the FBI.

No one is listening. Everyone seems programmed like ants on an ant hill in the jungle, oblivious to anything or the complex world but the anthill before them. No one is listening. No one cares, and the media has them all programmed and twisted to think the same. There was no happiness or meaning in saving anyone after his attempts to warn the public as disappointment set in Geo.

CHAPTER 13

MARXISMS

Geo decides to take Mina's cryptic hand written note to the local police department sergeant to try to protect Mina. Sergeant Wilcox said he would look into it. Mina ended up dead the next day; her body was found beaten, ravaged, raped, and left to hang naked in a ritualistic position in the Cosmo Place Alley parking lot a block away the Boho Grove. Geo read the murder was under investigation. Geo is fuming.

As Geo ruminates in horror that in his effort to protect Mina, his interference executed her imminent death. Looking outside of himself Geo takes his rage out on the system. In San Francisco, it may take many years to find justice for Mina's murder. There is no one to defend her, except Geo. Welcome Geo, to the Land of the Free, Home of the Brave, socialism permeated every facet of the legal system from police, to judges and attorneys.

All the local police departments have been defunded, influenced by extreme leftist ideologies and pressured by corrupted nonprofit black socialist activist groups rioting, burning down and destroying city after city in mainly democratic cities and states, founded by black trained lesbian godless Marxist organizers who were formally trained by gay male Caucasian socialist trainers vetted by the CIA, alongside a defuncted sold out corrupt mayor and a Marxist corrupt district attorney who previously worked as a translator for the Marxist leader of Venezuela Hugo Chavez. This exiled corrupt district attorney and people like Nara paid illicit nonprofits with favorable donations which guaranteed their status and protected them socially and publicly. 90% of the nonprofit organizations in San Francisco have socialistic tendencies funded by wealthy misguided global nonprofit elitist using philanthropy as a veil to hide under while they insidiously planted socialistic people in power and illicit laws to protect them every step of the way including other well-known Non-governmental Organizations (NGOs). One of these elitists gives billions to these fake nonprofits to ruin American from the bottom up and from the top down, corrupting politicians at the top and causing divide with the public at the bottom. The destructive socialist plan is called "Top-Down, Bottom-Up, Side to Side". It was created to control people and to destroy freedom and replace it with socialism in America by all means.

Their core values shifted to a Marxist system in the name of philanthropy in exchange for multi-million-dollar donations, largely untaxed through donation nonprofit tax schemes. Most of these nonprofits were hijacked. Even the "Alphabet Salad" gay nonprofits, originally created for gay civil liberties in the 1970s now represented socialistic values and tendencies which its original founders never intended and are now manipulated and guided by insidious CIA and the FBI, shoving little dull and unoriginal gay rainbows down everyone's throats with daily propaganda. On the surface, the public thought these organizations were all philanthropic and offered some utopian value for society, yet they sold themselves out to a greater Marxist agenda sporting little bland communist fist as their icons to posture to everyone their prominent position and control in San Francisco's government.

Trying to achieve any sort of Justice for Mina would be virtually impossible. They were all in on it, as each group, directly or indirectly, supported each other's group for worse and worse. No one would ever know the truth and secrets Mina knew and wished to reveal to save her life. And how many women in that brothel and innocent victims has this happened to?

The local police department is also corrupt in the upper echelons of power. Crime across the board has risen 65% since the new corrupt black female leftist mayor and her lover Nara was elected, rather hand-picked, as San Francisco's Mayor conveniently after the murder and fall of the previous coveted Chinese mayor.

CHAPTER 14

PYRAMIDION

Disappointed and discouraged at everyone, Geo turns to his Kwoon. He enters the Kwoon and sits in the middle of the patio to mediate.

Li appears next to him. Geo explains to him what the Elites want to do. Geo gets very detailed about how they planned the biggest bank heist in human history, but it gets worse. He explains to Li how his position as a Notary has put him in a place where he has gathered much knowledge of what corporations, secret societies, and the elites in San Francisco and the world are planning to do.

Li listens quietly.

Geo continues how they are interconnected because although it seems like a mess of information, people, and groups, there is a definite order to all the madness. At first, when Geo started to gather information from the sources, notary client after client after client from all different directions, Geo cracked the code. There is a hierarchy Geo explains. It is like a triangle but more like a pyramid. Geo believes this structure has been around for quite some time, maybe hundreds of years or more, judging by the documents shuffled in the notarizations. Geo explains that it looks like the pyramid on the American one-dollar bill. More like a pyramid with many complex layers of bricks and stones representing many layers of people, federal and state judges, prosecutors, groups, politicians, actors, corporations, and secret societies, and many of San Francisco's wealthy were part of these layers. Every layer above has more power and authority than the layer below all the way to the top cornice of the pyramid.

Each layer carries out a specific order and narrative from the layer above to accomplish the overall narrative coded within the highest pyramidion cap layer. Every layer can mix to assist any other layer in conveying and putting the main narrative forth. The lowest layer is the normal naïve, public taking all the weight at the bottom and holding the entire structure together unknowingly and innocently, yet holding the same amount of responsibility for the narrative. Ignorance is never an excuse from responsibility, and therefore the lower layer will also be implicated in whatever narrative the pyramidion creates.

Li listens steadily.

As the layer moves to the top, there are fewer people in that layer, establishing that group's importance. The layer before the pyramidion is a group of 13 vital people in this pyramid Council of 13.

There have been many documents notarized by this Council of 13 and I am seeing unusual things like FEMA-styled camps being built in the Dogpatch district with many plastic caskets being ordered and fencing and blockading materials. I saw a document that fencing was to be built continuously to the South Side of the City boundary with a privately hired group of missionary militias to guard the perimeter. Something is definitely going on here. I notarized a general contractor's construction contract to build a basement, but the plans look more like an underground bomb shelter for a wealthy couple in Pacific Heights. I have been notarizing all sorts of suspicious documents, and I am concluding that there is a narrative that they are planning to round people up and do whatever they plan to do with people, Geo explains.

Many documents were created in Switzerland and notarized here in San Francisco. Some of the documents are from Venice, Italy. The documents are uniquely made, unlike regular paper and the thick ink also smells like blood.

Li breaks his silence, "Venice? What do you know about

Venice?" Geo responds, "I only know that there was a huge money transfer in the multi-millions transferred to a city official personally yesterday from Venice, Italy, via Switzerland and the transfer seemed highly irregular and suspect. Li asks, "May I add some wisdom, Geo?" Geo excitedly says, "Sure shoot!" Li continues, "Let me ask you a question. Did the pasta noodle come from China or Italy?" Geo squints, "China?" Li smiles, "No one really knows. History is often murky and always twisted to fit the conqueror's agenda. The truth is it all depends on what type of food you like most, Italian or Chinese? But my great-grandfather Ru-Ping, told me a story when I was very young. I learned when I got older that he was a great storyteller after he would have a few hits of Opium!

Before I continue, I want you to know Geo that you have been indoctrinated all of your life since you were born. Indoctrinated by first your parents. Schools, peers, the educational system, colleges, and so on. No one knew better but to copy what they learned by tradition, and no one ever asked where the tradition came from. Then that tradition is packaged in a television marketing campaign for you and your family to buy more goods and feel good about yourself. If Santa Claus was fabricated by the Coke Corporation in the 1950's, why would it be so hard to believe me?"

Geo agrees and says, "I always felt something was not right about me. I never felt right in my shoes. I just do things because I have to do them for no reason. I work hard to be successful, then when I reach the top of success, it all flees, and things do not make sense, and it's like a maze that I run over and over again. I see time passing, I am getting older, and I feel like I am in a program I cannot awaken from."

Li Mi says, "Geo since you're begging the question, have you ever heard of the saying: *Who controls the past controls the future. Who controls the present controls the past?*" Geo cringes, "Li, is someone controlling us?" Li says, "Let me explain: You may be ready for what I have to say in light of everything you have told me and discovered. These truths are unknowns that are known, and it is a fact that we have been lied to over and over again, not for decades but for centuries. A global falsification of history Geo, of epic proportions. Like you, I have also sought the truth, and the truth has found me through you Geo." Li starts laughing uncontrollably. "And it all makes sense now. Geo, my forefathers, come from Beijing, formally known as Peking China."

CHAPTER 15

INEFFABLE GOD

"Geo, before I indulge in Peking, I have a question for you. Do you have faith in anything? A place, a person, a spirit, or something ultimately ineffable?"

Geo looks down through the large circular window as he watches Li's Win Chung warriors train and spar in the central Dojo. One warrior catches his eye by the name of Lyu Lopez, a pretty Chilean woman, a short but aggressively strong warrior, as she thrusts her palms against another warrior's chest. Geo watches as her opponent flies across the bamboo floor mats. He hits the wall and faints. Lyu bows down, refocuses, and sits to meditate. Lyu's strength, expressed in her fierce eyes, arouses Geo's curiosity.

The monks in the Dojo gather the beat laid-out warrior and lay him in a copper tub full of a thick gooey liquid made from a core mixture of honey. Another monk in an all-white robe sits at the corner glass cubical as he plays a brass singing bowl at a frequency of 250hz. Geo silently muses that he looks like an ancient DJ who has mastered his art. Geo listens to the soothing continuous low vibrational hum resonating through the Dojo. The monk chants in unfamiliar vocabulary as Lyu leaves the sparring mat and respectfully exits the Dojo. Other monks gather and surround the warrior to perform what look like katas, yet their movements are much smoother, non-aggressive, and choreographed precisely to this hypnotic humming. They look like they are floating, lighter than the air around them.

Geo's gaze moves toward light beaming from a small structure within the glass cubical. It looks like a miniature shining stupa on a Moorish-styled temple, assembled with four granite limestone blocks on each side with an inner copper lining and a 24k gold shell. The stupa is held up by four solid gold rods propped upward from each block to hold the stupa like a roof. Laser lights are flickering towards the middle of the gold rods with clips. It is a digital spectrum analyzer that measures and reads frequency measurements, almost like a biofeedback device.

A monk in a red gown enters the Dojo, presenting a beehive attached to a brass rolling pedestal. He sedates the hive with smoke made of pine needles. He carefully locates one of the worker bees and clips the bee's abdomen to the geometric center of the stupa's gold rods. As the bee buzzed, the laser lights transmitted the physical energy generated by the bees' wings to a small digital converter at the bottom of this contraption. This sound amplified into the Dojo, integrating with the singing bowl harmonic converting the frequency to heal the wounded martial arts warrior.

Geo turns his thoughts back to Li's inquisition about the ineffable.

"Yes, Geo, we heal our warriors with sound frequencies. The low hum you hear is played at the exact frequency of a honey bee as it flaps its wings. At 250hz, the bees form the honeycombs, where bees store their precious honey within the beehive. They are formed into squares, triangles, or hexagons, depending on slight speed variations of that tiny bee's magnificent wing beat, creating those specific frequencies.
Can you imagine that, Geo? This is why honey is used to heal, sweeten, beautify the body, and many other amazing things. As humans, we also have a specific frequency ranging from 4-7.5hz, and so does the earth at 7.83hz. Everything has a frequency. Frequencies are instrumental to our mission Geo. It can also be used as a fierce weapon when needed. But the bees and the ancients used it to build homes and places that store energy, just like honey. You will learn more if we move forward.

Now tell me, Geo, is there an ineffable God?

Geo explains, "My mother Graciela once told me how she met my father. She came from an impoverished Mexican family in Casa Grande, Spanish for grand *houses.* Also known as Paquimé, it is a ruin prehistoric archaeological site in the northern parts state of Chihuahua. It is believed that the construction of the site is originally attributed to a Mongolian culture.

No one knows who built the site, but the native inhabitants moved in. Some say the place is anywhere from 3000 to 9000 BC years old. As a child, when we would visit my grandmother on vacation, I remember my brothers and sister holding my hands and crossing me over 3-foot-wide ancient water canals built by the ancient inhabitants of these historic Casa Grande Ruins. It was a hot Ancient Mexican desert town with many complicated archeological ruins.

My mother, Grace, was born in 1940 and experienced a tragic childhood. My grandfather, Francisco, her father, was murdered. He was a furniture mover, and a Mexican cartel mistook him for another cartel gangster and shot him dead in the middle of the street in front of his moving truck. Soon my mother's family went poor. There was one instance where they didn't have anything to eat, so they would suck on ice cubes and pretend it was food; that is how bad it had gotten for her. It was heartbreaking for me to hear her say this. There were no jobs in the small desert town, so her brothers convinced my mother to sell her body to other men to put food on the table for the family, and she did. She was forced to commit evil to survive and sacrificed herself and her soul for her family. Men have failed my mother all her life; therefore, she always sought God. She became Catholic and found no salvation in the unfulfilling religion, so she turned to the Jehovah's Witnesses, only to be left even lonelier. Finally, she found a relationship with Jesus, just as King David, the father of King Solomon, also found. She would dance to God, sing, pray, and treat God just like King David was purported to do. To her, Jesus, son of God, was the only Man that did her right and did right by her and her children. Living in a world with no control, Jesus empowered her, and she raised five children on her own. When she finally tired of the abusive

MR. HECTOR OMAR ALDANA

regime, my father, she headed West to California. She finally found a way to forgive the life she was given. As she was growing up and trying to escape that impoverished Mexican town, she met my father. He was an American Mexican alcoholic who had dealings with the Mexican cartels. He gave her nothing more than children and an evil life of abuse. The only upswing was that Salvador gave her legal passage to the United States via marriage. Still, it cost her. Salvador, my father, had spent many years in jail for shooting and wounding two police officers right before he married my mother. He was fractured, a broken man his entire life, like a piece of unamended broken wood. He had met evil and became evil, and those evil spirits within him would eventually hurt everyone around him, and he released his pain to my mother. Salvador had nothing but evil demons to contend with and had brought the world of evil to my mother. In the end, my father passed. He lost his mind with no salvation. My mother survived; to this day, she still prays, dances, and sings to God.

So, to answer your question, Li. I do not believe in God. I am not religious. I don't go to church. I did experience good and evil in my life, and I see the difference. I see God in my mother and honor her God indirectly. Unfortunately, evil reaches me from time to time, because of my father's affiliations in El Paso with the cartels. I have street credibility because of my father's legacy, and my relatives reach out to seduce me with money. So, my mom's sacrifice keeps me on the good side of the tracks here. I believe my father's evil legacies go even further back in time when the Aztecs and Mayans ruled Mexico. There has always been a certain sense of brutality in Mexico. A vein of evil blood in the veins of that country keeps Mexico's people at bay and in constant fear for thousands of years. The Aztecs, Toltecs, and Mayans found every pious reason to murder and sacrifice children and others for the sake of their Gods, and the payment of someone else's blood was their virtue as it is in many evil religions.

These family lineages still in our bloodlines somehow

keep evil alive. So, I tend to see God in my mother. I see the goodness in her and would prefer a world reflected in her vision of things.

Geo: "So, I do believe in an ineffable God Li!"

Li: "Ah, I can sense your struggle between good and evil, Geo."

Geo sighs. "Yeah."

Li: "Geo, do you know the difference between a belief and faith?"

Geo: "I didn't know there was a difference, Li!"

Li:

1.   Do you believe in an ineffable God? Or...
2.   Do you have faith in an ineffable God?

Geo, there is a difference. It is said that, "Faith is not the absence of doubt, but rather faith keeps believing even in the midst of your doubts. Remember that faith is more than seeing. Faith is more than observable facts" It is impossible to quantify faith in any way. People who have religion believe in a God, but people who have faith have a relationship with God. Can you see the difference? Your mother has Faith in an Ineffable God, Geo!

"YES, I SEE! Yet I don't know if I have faith like my mother; at this point I suppose I am a believer, Li."

"Well, at least now you see the difference, Geo."

"Yes. I do now. Thank you, Sensi!"

You have a choice, Geo. You can see the world pragmatically, based on science, facts, and statistics, down to the atom, neutrino, nano God particles or as in the large Hadron collider at CERN; a new discovery with every collision.

"Or you can choose to see the world with a different lens. For Example:

Choose to see the world through science and technology; you will find antidotes, formulas, processes, and more technology but have yet to find answers. And if you need any healing or salvation, if you take that track, you are doomed.

Scientists and physicians have no cure for mental

illnesses. At one point in time, they were cutting portions of the brain out to treat people, scientifically called lobotomies, leaving these souls brain-dead like zombies to cure them. Happened every day at asylums like Agnew's Hospital. Today they treat mental illness and all illnesses with drugs and more drugs to combat all of the side effects that each drug produces, causing drug addictions. Geo! No one has ever been cured this way. What kind of mad science is this and who could lay their trust in it?

Pharmaceutical companies are the biggest drug dealers. This is the business of pharmaceuticals. These people see the world and its problems pragmatically, and society believes in them. Pharmaceutical companies love making billions of dollars and fooling people rooted in their belief in their doctors. These people believe doctors will have the cure for cancer and all the health problems in the world today. Yet good doctors who know the truth, know they can't help heal their patients are censured, neglected, abused and shun by the system too.

Geo, the world is full of people trying to fix problems, we create technologies and mechanical things that break down and cause more problems, and people run faster to fix everything. Faster cars, faster computers, faster software, faster lives, faster education, faster technology. How fast is fast enough? And now they want to imbed people with tiny little digital mental computers with AI software technology to make people efficient, smarter, and faster?

Even the food we eat is synthetic. The homes we build are synthetic. With no rhyme, reason, answers, and ultimately no meaning, Geo. We solve a problem here only to have bred 10 more problems there. Pragmatics Geo!! In the end, people end up with material things that don't matter at the end of the day. When you believe Geo, the answers ultimately leave you empty, even if you pass this life believing, when we instantly know this isn't the right way. Some worship it to their own demise.

Geo, do not get me wrong, Artificial Intelligence (AI) Crypto Currency, Blockchain Technology, medicine, your smartphone, and your Mac or PC, even the Snap-on Wrench or

Milwaukee Saw are good for us, but at the same time, they are merely tools nothing more and nothing less. Are your XRPP crypto tokens that made you rich now better for you?

Society and corporations want to substitute these mere tools as your fundamental way of living and as Gods to rule and control lives. The more they figure out ways to get these tools into your finances, body and soul, the more control they will have over you to try to fix the problems they created. And you lose your being and your freedoms along the way. This is the long game in the end. This is the resultant if you mix and melt it all in caldron. Or you can see the world in a different way Geo!

As Li explains, he becomes more aggressive and closer to Geo's face. Geo is surprised and almost scared as Li sways in his demeanor. Why are you still listening to me, Geo? Why are you still here, Geo? You are better now, and you have no reason to be here? Why Geo?

Which is it, Geo? Will you have faith or a belief?"

The monk's humming sound becomes more intense throughout the dojo playing at frequency of 528hz.

"Li, I want to have more than belief. Everything I see today is so corrupt, so, so evil, so old, so dull, so stale. Nothing surprises me anymore. I used to think that having a great career, family and friends, vacations, cars, Rolex watches, and everything material to support my entire mindset was everything. Now it has no value Li. I see people pass, and it's like they never lived at all. So meaningless. So empty inside. I love my daughter and want her near me, but nothing I can do, even to restore the past, will make any difference now. I know now that no matter what I do as a father, my legacy will have the same thoughts as I do in the end. She will be empty, too, and I have no control over that, Li. To her, I may as well be dead.

Don't get me wrong, Li, I am not fatal, and I am not suicidal; it is just that anything that this material world produces is always headed in one direction, and at the end of it all, it has no favorable meaning; some laughs, some happiness, intermixed with sadness. Not even charitable acts do me well. I haven't given up on my life. I am still here, am I not? I am making the best of it, but I am merely going through the strokes, knowing that there is something I am missing here. I want change Li, but a meaningful change.

It is like I am chasing my tail, and the more I chase, the more lifeless I become. It is a vicious cycle. I don't even hate my enemies anymore. I want to have faith Li, but I know that everything this life and world have to offer is in a state of entropy. It is always coming undone that it is a miracle we live at all. I did the math, and it doesn't add up. Yet I do want faith. I see no resolution without it."

"Prove it to me. Prove it to yourself, Geo!"

The constant hum gets more intense.

"How Li?"

"You are absolutely right, Geo. This world was made and is in a state of entropy, and it is a miracle that we live. Anything living right now goes against this state of entropy in this fabric of time. Can you imagine the amount of energy this entropy has mounted against the universe? Yet we defy all those odds and get a chance to live. How is it so if not a miracle?

Ultimately, we get to live a mere moment because that force was made to conquer us? We will pass defiantly. We will wrinkle, and bones will be scattered eventually. Some people live one day, some 100 years, and some pass right before us. What we did yesterday may or may not matter today. We have no idea what it will bring. So only now matters. You are here now, and you never imagined that you would be here with me, Geo. So, time is not of the essence whether we live one or 100 years. There is no fairness here. The clock stops here and now. Scientists can't even define what time is. We only use it as a tool of measurement, right. So, if everything is in a state of entropy, things rust and break, and time doesn't matter, what else is left?"

"I see where you are going with this, Li."

"So, what is left, Geo?

"Faith Li."

"Exactly Geo!"

Li continues, "You can be here one year or 100 years, be like Mother Teresa or Gandhi and exhibit acts of kindness, or be a serial killer, a murderer, or whatever you deem that will make your menial time worthwhile on earth. It doesn't matter. Everything will become rust and dust in the end. The math! We are here merely to believe or to have faith in an ineffable God.

And once you choose, everything you do is no different from what you have done in the past. You let yourself go to the will of this ineffable God. There are no questions, no answers, no logic. Our only goal in our present life and now is to say yay, or nay to this ineffable God. The rest is up to God's will.

We make a plan, but we still have a choice. We have to make the best of it. So, let's kick the shit out of these people planning mayhem upon us. Hopefully, this is God's will, yet we will pray on it. Prove it to me, Geo. Prove to me that you have faith!

"Who is this God, Li?"

"The same God that created you, Geo! God doesn't have a bible. People do. A religion does not constitute a God merely a set of traditions and guidelines. The God that created everything, Geo. The God that created you and me. The God that has you believing this world has no ultimate value, but your choice to seek him does. It is a binary choice, a one or zero, yay or nay. Yet you still know there is far better in store for you. That God Geo.

Some people believe there is a hell, but if you do not pass this test, it won't matter. You can take the test, and no harm will be done, other than if you fail, you just keep living in the same world. Yet, if you pass, I can guarantee your vision will open widely. You will understand the same
world but in a very different way than you do now. Your imagination will be empowered to open to an unknown depth between you and your God." The humming stops.

CHAPTER 16

FAITH VERSUS BELIEF

Li points north toward two red Teutonic-shaped 12-foot-tall doors adorned with forged iron rusted plates and rivets. Geo, you've come to the fork in the labyrinth. When life's circumstances misplace you, immoral and evil people cross your path. Your hard work ethic fuels your quest to return to the life you once had and to regain the connection you lost with your daughter. You were smart enough to connect the dots, leading to your destiny here. With me, Geo. You are on your way to finding your path again.

Although you have learned about these nefarious secret entities and evil secret societies and what they wish to do, you are now in a quandary. You have witnessed the demons in people and now know what true evil looks like. Even as a child, Geo, you have experienced evil people and know what depravity feels like.

You never suspected those circumstances forced on you by wicked people set you up to fail, indirectly and directly, ultimately leading you astray from your true calling -- to accept the loving heavenly person you are. Your body, inside and out, bears the unbidden scars of these illicit events in your lifetime, so you would ultimately surrender your spirit to goodness and God.

Demons, Geo, sometimes look like monsters in the movies, yet in their presence, when you look into their beady eyes, you can even smell their sulfurous odors. Demons never answer your questions. They only probe for weakness and use it against you. So, most people are not immune to evil; they partake in the conspiracy without understanding what they are getting into. They were born into it all, so how would they know the difference? Especially as a child? Of course, you couldn't. But now, Geo, your eyes are awakening. Like all the others, you felt it all your life, but today, you will fully awaken to the truth.

You know a lot now, Geo. You saw Mina perish, and in due time, others will, too. You saw them sign their names in blood; you administered oaths and affirmations to them and acknowledged their dastardly deeds.

Sometimes, Geo, we are complicit in the crimes of others even without agreeing to the crime. Still, we unwittingly accept equal responsibility for the crime because we have accepted survival. We are all guilty, complicit, compliant, comfortable, and complacent.

You have their names written in your journals. You know their faces and where they abide. You were not supposed to know any of this, but you fell through the cracks and became naively aware. Now, you put yourself in a role of surveillance, gathering intelligence and information about people, places, and evil things. No one could have been in a better offense or defense position, yet you remain unnoticed. You are an enigma. You are a private "spy" without an agenda, sparked by your curiosity at what the mad world has concocted, and you just tripped into it as a Notary.

But no one will listen to you, Geo! Everyone is in the program, but you fell out somehow, and no one can relate to you anymore. Worse, you are a liability to people, your friends and family, and much more to yourself. You know too much! Even your Harvard attorney tried to shut you up. Yes, the very same attorney who signed a notarized oath with his legal name to honor the US Constitution. Yet he was the first to expurgate you. Why Geo? Why?

Like fools, they chase their tail and bite off the tails of others when they feel threatened. They allow their competitive egos to grow like fat balloons that pop the minute they are humiliated by the truth. Is this progress? They are sophisticatedly programmed.

From their Tesla's to their Mac's to their iPhones, they are sucked into whatever program that does not conflict with their tidy survival. And to survive, they must trump the success of others, believing that they must do malicious things to others to win and to survive. Civilization after civilization, history only shows their demise. At least all are smart enough to destroy themselves.

Now you have either a big or small problem, Geo. The question is, do you want to do something about it?

Geo, I have mentored you back to health, and I want to have faith in you, yet this is a new beginning for you, whichever way you choose. As you have become strong, I will no longer be your mentor. I can do nothing more to add value to your life, and I have other students to mentor.

As is fated, I have major undertakings soon, Geo. You can fall back into your programmed life by walking out of here this very moment, Geo. Soon, you will earn what you lost in every which way and forget all about everything that has transpired here. You will be back in the program with the rest of them again. And yes, you will be the father you wish to be with your daughter, Summer. Everything will return to the reality that was yours in the past.

You are welcome to stay a few more weeks to close out you're training. Just walk out the door behind me.

Geo looks at the door behind Li and then looks back at the red Teutonic doors.

"Li, I want to be a good father! I look at how badly things fell apart in every bit of my life, and I know threading to the past will not make me a better father or offer anything of great value to my daughter, family, friends, or even society. After what I have seen and been through, this secular life here on earth is not my destiny. The world is a mess: funded riots, nefarious organizations burning down cities posing as nonprofits, philanthropists who are nothing less than satanic. I have seen these documents with my own eyes here in San Francisco. It looks like a war zone out there! Nonprofits hand out Fentanyl to people drug-hinged like zombies living in tents on the streets. Police feed them Narcan to keep them from dying, and the same process repeats daily to get more funding. These nonprofits here in San Francisco are operated literally by people who worship Satan on Sundays. San Francisco is the capital of Satanist worship. They must feed evil into drug addicts and conveniently call them homeless to pull people's heartstrings for their socialist governmental payoffs and programs.

The drug addicts don't need homes; they want drugs, and the pharmaceuticals are nothing but legalized drug dealers with big fat mansions and homes in the better districts of San Francisco, and their attorneys who live in Marin and northern coastal cities are all peddling liberalism and Utopian socialistic lifestyles for all but themselves. The drug addicts are not homeless per se. Pharma makes them addicts at the taxpayer's expense. Lend a hand to do better for one of the drug addicts, and attorneys will sue you for interfering. Without addicts, nonprofits wouldn't raise any money.

I am signing millions of dollars' worth of invoices paid to these nonprofits, and their leadership all in on it, signing their names in blood. They will not solve the problem but will feed the fuel of San Franciscan's hearts with their lies. If this isn't evil at a spiritual level, it is evil wrapped in a secular world and happening mainly in liberal states, but no one is immune to this malfeasance.

So, what are the globalists doing? Globalist own the pharmaceuticals and their CEO's wives run the nonprofits. These leaders that are tied to the cabal are carpetbagging billions of dollars and selling America's freedoms, pointing fingers at everyone but own liberals. It is genius.

Drug trafficking at the Mexican/American borders, child and human trafficking, evil everywhere I look, and now I know where it all comes from! Structured behind people's backs, and the worst part that the public is willfully oblivious. The news feeds their intellectual ego like hungry varmints. And I am Mexican!

It looks like a facade to me. A dragon's mask! Things do not make sense at all! I do the math, and nothing adds up. There are disparities everywhere I look. And these disparities are created to control people.

When I go back in history, I see more bad than good. Civilizations coming and going. How much good are we humans doing if history repeats itself in the most God-awful ways? Another civilization gone! There is nothing beyond that door behind you that I seek, Li. Yes, I know too much."

Tears of anger flow from Geo's eyes.

"Who are "They" Li?

"Would it surprise you, Geo, that when Russia invaded Ukraine, the Orthodox Cathedral church of Odessa was bombed along with other Tartaria designed UNESCO-protected Neo-Classical Beaux-arts buildings? It appears that war after war, from World War 1 to wars in Iraq, Afghanistan, and Iran, the first buildings to be blown to pieces are the historically significant buildings and artifacts with these Tartarian symmetries.

I don't think Putin bombed these buildings ironically, as Ukraine's leader Vladimir Zelensky has been trying to eliminate all of the Christian types of religions from his country, making it look like Russia bombed these buildings. Zelensky has been ethnically cleansing Ukraine and Ukrainian citizens with his Neo-Nazi faction the Azov's in Crimea, killing Christians or jailing them along with devout Christian Ukrainians, not to mention forcing any Ukrainian young men, women and adult male and females to fight in his globalist useless war. Ukraine has always been a bed of controversy since the holocaust, and the same Neo Nazis have remained in part of that country, making Ukraine one of the most corrupt places on earth, not to mention all the human trafficking that goes on there. Even the current corrupt president's crackhead son had his share of Ukrainian crack whores and parties there, according to his famous lost and recovered laptop within his Ukrainian Bioweapons company Rosemont Seneca, None the less the actual neo-classic Tartarian-type buildings are the first to be destroyed in every war. Thy are trying to hide history by destroying Tartarian ancient buildings.

The bombings of this church and other beaux-art buildings were definitely inside jobs by Zelensky as it turns out that Putin practices Orthodox Christianity and Putin tends to respect Tartarian kinds of structures and history as Putin opened the doors and unsealed the older Tartarian maps locked away in Russian Achieves to the public in 2015. Putin is uncovering the truth about history. The liberal progressive minds in the US hate this truth.

I don't think Putin has it in his heart to bomb what he believes in. In fact, I believe Putin knows much more than I do on this subject and the doors to knowledge about Tartaria are opening wide.

One has to be crazy to believe the mass media regarding this war, as Americans have given over $120 billion to Zelensky and his military cronies to pocket. His generals are buying mansions and exotic sports cars and lining their pockets with these funds. But one thing that stands out is that in every war, these fantastic Tartarian buildings get obliterated conveniently by war, fire, or some form of natural disaster. The US Air Force, coupled with the Department of Defense (DOD) with Raytheon Technologies and Lockheed Martin, has created the perfect fire-breathing dragon called LANCE.

Many people believe that the LANCE laser has been burning down many areas claimed as natural fire disasters. Of course, this is merely a conspiracy theory for now.

And it isn't funny that in March of 2022, Russian Artist and architect Ekaterina Polyakova built a huge 65-foot-tall model of the Tower of Babel for the annual Maslenitsa festival in Russia to pose a warning to the world about a coming nuclear war driven by the WESF's Clause Schwapp and the satanic United Nations, New World Order and other NGOs now. Russia's and Putin's defiance of a One World Government, just like Nimrod had during the days of Babylon building the actual Tower of Babel in defiance and Fear of God's Promise.

That mock wooden tower of babel was burned to the ground in Russia. It was a marvelous sight to see Geo, and then Russia reluctantly invaded Ukraine and the UN's encroachment on the Russian borders and territory, even though Zelensky had a signed agreement with Putin for peace right until the new US president became involved and pushed Ukraine to warring Russia. The One World Order, which is constantly pushed by Klaus Schwab, uses Americans and America's 120-billion funding and military equipment as their money to illicitly encroach on Russia's sovereign border. What is more unbelievable is that Zelensky is prancing in women's heels, begging for more funding while he jails his own people and while Nancy Pelosi, Sean Penn, and Bono have a concert in the middle of this so-called Russia invasion. They later paired to perform a live concert at the very beginning of the war. Not to mention Hunter and Beau Biden's investments in bioweapons companies like Rosemont Seneca and Burisma. Nonetheless, these magnificent buildings are being systematically destroyed, war in and war out, and the gothic Odesa Orthodox church was bombed to bits and pieces.

They are hiding the truth of the potential of these structures and the truths they hide within, and now, today, you find yourself in the middle of one of these great architectural structures, Geo.

Geo, I did not build those red Teutonic doors or the Tartarian dome. The dome was here when my great-great-grandfather Ru-Ping came to work on building the Union Pacific Railroad in the 1860s as an indentured laborer from Peking, China. The Railroads corporations worked the Chinese ruthlessly with very little hope for a future.

My great-great-grandfather struck a vane of gold in Northern California after setting explosives in a train tunnel, revealing larger gold fragments scattered throughout the tunnel before anyone noticed him. A few other Chinese laborers took enough bags of gold nuggets to buy out their debts and their freedom. They bought this import-export-trading warehouse in Chinatown and other properties in San Francisco. His small group paid the price of labor and humiliation in this new free country, which taught them a lesson of humility. They created a benevolent secret society here in Chinatown. Most Chinese here at the time had no notion they existed. Before prohibition, tunnels were dug under all of Chinatown that last until this day. Chinese would trade underground, and they protected their own within these tunnels when we had to. Things were not fair back then either, and everything was done covertly.

It was said that there was a larger Tartarian Beaux-Arts, neo-classic building here before the import-export warehouse that I converted into this dojo. My grandfather used the warehouse as a front for a Chinese import trading business, a cash cow to fund his benevolent group -- no different than the nonprofits you speak of now, but our intentions were quite different.

The original building was very difficult to demolish, and the megalithic foundations are still embedded in the ground. No one has yet to discover who demolished the building and why. Someone said it was a magnificently large building and that some company arbitrarily demolished these preexisting buildings in San Francisco before the new inhabitants migrated here in the 1850s. So, it is said the buildings were constructed anywhere from the 1200's to the 1800's. There is no recorded history, only legends.

The Yelamu (Ramaytush), a sect of the Ohlone tribe of Native Americans, were indigenous people believed to be here in San Francisco for at least 13,500 years Geo. They were considered the "Mound People" as they would build huge shell mounds, some up to 30-50 feet high, for spiritual ceremonies and other purposes. The Spanish Catholic missionaries tore their culture to pieces in 1777, as the Cortez did with the Montezuma and the Mechicas in Azteca, now Mexico City, in the 1500s. That being said, this Tartarian dome here and other specific structures were not built by the Yelumu; they were created by someone or an entity that is a mystery to us. This

Dome is proof, as you will see. For some reason, the dome was hidden and survived destruction. Even the Yelamu's 425 shell mounds were destroyed except for two in the Bay Area.

Who destroyed them or why? No one knows. Yet, a current theme is that someone or something was trying to hide the truth. No one ever knows who destroys this hidden history.

When my great-grandfather decided to build a tunnel 200 feet into the Earth, this large open room appeared that we are standing in now. They were in disbelief to find a structured spacious room, and then, in the dark, they stumbled onto the red Teutonic doors leading into the Dome. My great-grandfather had providence for luck, and his secret benevolent society was inspired by a new vision with this finding. Somebody or some entity hid this Dome from the world. And we found it by chance, maybe by destiny.

So, Geo, who built it and why? I have searched high and low to discover the truth. Many copycat architects designed similar buildings throughout San Francisco in the early 1900s after a convenient fire burned the city and this neighborhood down. I can see some fake neo-classic buildings only a few blocks away, but I wonder if the copycat Tartarian buildings have anything like we do here.

Most of these architects studied at Ecole des Beaux-Arts school in France, a design college created over 350 years ago that fundamentally taught the basic architectural design rules created by the Greeks, Romans, Egyptians, and Nubians. These techniques extrapolated older architectural designs noted in the Book of Solomon and how his temple was constructed. It goes back to how the first brick was engineered to build the Tower of Babel.

In 1915, George W. Kelham, a notable architect in San Francisco who studied Ecole Beaux-Arts, was the lead architect in charge of the Panama-Pacific International Exposition in San Francisco. He was the lead architect for many amazingly unique beaux-design commercial and residential buildings in San Francisco. Still, they appear to be architectural design remnants and echoes of the past. Still, I believe George was a member of a secret Masonic-type society carrying out a forbidden truth in his time. But current buildings are merely echoes of the past. They were mimicking a style of architecture, remnants of the true Tartarian structures like the pyramids discovered all over the world.

However, a few original buildings are still in San Francisco, and they may have tunnels and domes built into their catacombs. The Los Angeles Times reported that a geological mining engineer, G. Warren Shufelt, found mysterious catacombs 250 feet under Spring Street and North Broadway on Sunset Boulevard in Los Angeles in the 1930s. A local Native Indian Hopi legend is that lizard people lived in those tunnels for 5,000 years before the find. It was an intelligent race that banked stashes of gold in the walls.

It was reported in the *San Francisco Chronicle on* 10 June 1912, Page 8. in Concord, 50 miles from here, a 7.4-foot Native Indian was found by William Altmann, a curator for The Golden Gate Memorial Museum.

Yes, Geo, life on Earth is as surreal as the cosmos, like a giant Harry Potter book with strange beings and creatures. Artifacts prove it in drawings.

That is interesting, Li. Some of the people who signed notarized documents with me have awkward facial features that look lizard-like, but when I see them again, their features consistently change from appointment to appointment when I revisit them.

Geo, so perhaps these beings built the tunnel and domes here? Who knows. What I do know is if you enter the Dome, you will find something we call magical if you dare to do so.

Today, we see everything as technology. Our smartphones are technological advances, but what if we could all read each other minds? Would our natural ability be considered technology or merely a natural occurrence? So, Geo, what is the purpose of technology for us?

Li, technology is merely a tool for us to survive anything

that falls on Maslow's law of hierarchy.

Exactly Geo! Do you know what was the first recorded technological advancement of humans? No, I don't, Li.

Li continues, "The Talmud and other biblical historical books specify that because Adam and Eve experienced the feeling of being cold that they had never felt in the Garden, God granted them clothing made of sacrificial animals to keep them warm in their habitat after they were ejected from Eden and into the bittersweet cold and hot world. So, God gave humans the first technological advancement, and that is what we consider clothing today. It's only a small technology, but it was and still is a very effective tool for our survival. If you deem it spiritual, it covers Adam and Eve's shame for taking a bribe from Lucifer. Nonetheless, it was humanity's first form of technology."

"So, Li, what we perceive as technology can merely be considered a natural tool for our survival?"

Li continues, "Exactly! For some reason, we are sold on the idea of technological advancements. Everything that man creates, especially with wires, batteries, software, hardware, a power source, and a screen, is something to be revered as a technological advancement. And now we rely on those technology creators to dictate our future. So, all those advancements that are supposedly good for human beings come to us with a proprietary, trademarked, copyrighted technology at a cost. In the end, everything becomes dated, slow, useless, and eventually breaks down but merely to the financial benefit of the entity that trademarked it.

So yes, although these technological advancements help us in many different ways. We are not better off in the end. Every day, our governments threaten each other with nuclear technologies to defy all the technological tools they created. All technology humans build breaks down and is meant to break society down. Just look at this mRNA vaccine technology that world governments gave to its people. It's killing people over time and putting world governments in grave trillion-dollar debts.

Do birds, animals, and insects need technology to survive? Jets engines and airplanes are superior fighting technologies, but if you look at birds, they move much faster than jets proportionally with 90-degree turns in milliseconds. And what about the dragonfly! No human technology can ever fly like a dragonfly can. Yet, we believe that jets are technologically advanced. They are only heaps of metal and wires, but the wars don't end with this technology. Humans are on the wrong path to technology.

So, the technology end-game is to fear, encapsulate, enslave, and succumb humans to their control. A society does not need technology to survive. Even now, people like George Soros, Bill Gates, Dr. Anthony Fauci, and Klaus Schwab, The World Economic Forum (WEF), The World Health Organization (WHO), NATO, the United Nations, thousands of philanthropical nonprofit organizations and NGOs talk about population control. They use technology like mRNA vaccines and medicine, other technologies in the skies, and AI to curb the 8 billion lives on this Earth to under 3 billion inhabitants. Apparently, their copyrighted technology has produced too many human beings to control.

Yet the most fundamental technology that God created is still here with us today, and it kills no one.

No amount of human technology or algorithms will solve our problems. They only bring more problems. Most people waste their lifetimes in front of digital screens until their hair turns gray, and they miss living life until they retire old and wrinkled like worn leather boots. They miss the sand between their toes on aqua-blue beaches in exchange for faster electric gadgetry or whimsical, mentally dysfunctional, dysphoric apps on their smartphone. All that time was lost and given for a paycheck to pay their never-ending bills and credit cards with rewards points built in to pay for their cavalier, meaningless lifestyles with their next paycheck. They are deceiving themselves. They bought the lie.

Geo, you don't need technology to grow tomatoes, lettuce,

cucumbers, cattle, chickens, eggs, and even fruit to survive. You don't even need a bench press to be healthy.

But what if humans took the wrong technological route, Geo? What if they limited themselves to encased piles of copper wires, resistors, capacitors, transformers, inverters, silicon chips, quartz displays, software, hardware, artificial intelligence, useless algorithms, and now humanoid robots and brain implants?

Geo, we limit ourselves by believing that the technology humans created has all the answers. We are plugged into notions daily that everything is governed by technology. People are given Nobel prizes and treated like gods because they concocted such mad technologies. Along with all the technologies, doctors and pharmaceutical companies have created hundreds of new illnesses with hundreds of new drugs to cure them over just 25 years. Illnesses that never existed in the history of humans now exist. Even air freshener plug-in technologies are poisoning people along with new chemical technologies they are putting in your food and drinks. What a mess, Geo!

What about our innate human technology, Geo? Megalithic structures worldwide have been found without a logical means of how they were created. Obviously, there was some kind of technology involved. There has yet to be a conclusion on how megalithic stones were cut, made, transported, and set in place.

Can you connect the dots here to what you have witnessed as a Notary? The God-awful awkward people you have legally engaged with? Are they part of the same evil unifying underlying workings you have recently experienced?

Geo, so perhaps these beings built the tunnel and domes here? Who knows. Yet, if you enter the Dome, you will find something we call magical if you dare to do so.

Geniuses like Nikola Tesla believed that the pyramids were not only architectural buildings but served a higher purpose of transmitting an energy source in the ionosphere. Tesla saw the earth as a giant electrical generator because the world has a northern and southern magnetic pole, which governs all objects that generate a magnetic force.

People may call him a mad scientist, but guess what. Every electrical producing utility in your gas, electrical car, home, business, or commercial building that stores, generates, and delivers electricity bows to his technology and is used billions of times daily all over the world. Thomas Edison helped fund Tesla's electromagnetic tower project until Edison discovered that because the energy was a God-given, natural given energy source, he would not be able to monetize and control this newly found energy and Tesla's discovery like Edison's greed did with his electric generator and transformer and other technologies Tesla created working under Edison's corporations. JP Morgan legally stopped and barred Tesla from fully developing his electromagnetic tower technology, which led to Tesla's uneventful demise as a scientist. So, as you can see, Geo, what is a God-given right to energy, is controlled in every which way by greedy humans, but it doesn't mean that we are limited to Edison or greedy humans like this. The energy is still there and free to us as a natural tool and means of survival. Just like the cob of corn, or tomato and apple that sprouts from the earth, that life gives us to survive on. It is all there and free. What appears to be not free is our thoughts. We are programmed not to see these things before our very eyes. But this is a clear case that technology can be used for good and evil. And yes, it is always evil when humans want to control technology.

By the way, Geo, Tesla believed that there had been interstellar communications with him while he was building his electromagnetic tower in Colorado. Tesla had a notion that these entities that were in communication with him had been visiting the earth and mankind for 1000s of years, and some had theorized that these communications had led him to create some of Tesla's technological inventions.

So, the Mayan, Bosnian, Nubian, Egyptian, Honduran, North American, South American, Chinese, Nordic, Asian, European, and Antarctica pyramids and thousands of pyramids around the ancient world are believed by some to have been created as power energy sources. How these primitive cultures attained the knowledge to build these structures remains a mystery. Maybe they shared similar communications and visions as Tesla? I do have a few guesses. Although it may be egotistical to consider these cultures as technologically primitive by how we define technology today. Did they need wires and silicon chips to live productive, content, meaningful lives? Maybe not! Maybe their tech was cleaner and more efficient.

If you enter those red doors, Geo, do not think of what you see as technology but as a way of life. It could be God-given, just like the clothes on your back, or it could be given by something else. If you enter that dome with a clear mind, not all you see will illude some kind of technology. Do not look at it as some steamed punk'd human-made Frankenstein of wires and chipsets. It would help to see it as the norm so you may gain further insight.

In the Talmud, God could communicate telepathically to Adam and Eve, and it is often said that when alien abductions occur, the so-called Grey Aliens communicate with their captive subjects telepathically. So, is that a technology or merely an ability to be discovered or rediscovered by humans? If you think of wires and silicon chips, you restrict yourself to that level. It adds no value to our innate genius as natural beings bound by materialistic contraptions that rust and decay.

I do not have complete proof, nor do I need it, Geo, but someone, something, some entity built this dome along with all of the pyramids around the world, none limited by a software program or silicon chipsets.

But this dome here still lives. The only difference is here, behind those red doors, it is powered up and running. Therefore, we keep it a complete secret as we know what evil governments do with natural technologies like this. Now it is your secret too. Once you walk through those red doors, you will see Geo.

Li, what do you mean by Tartarian type of buildings?

What is Tartarian? Geo, when you walk up at the intersecting six points of Kearny, Columbus, and Pacific Streets on your way to my dojo in Chinatown, what unusual building do you see that sticks out like a Gothic structure?

Yes, Li, I have seen the ornate building on my way to my appointments between the FIDI and Chinatown in the Little Italy district. It's a neoclassic seven-story building covered in copper-clad valances and window coverings and includes a large copper domed stupa with these incredible green rusted patina window frames. Yes, exactly what we have been discussing.

Geo, that Sentential building is a copycat, an echoed remnant of what the Tartarian buildings looked like architecturally. That is a Tartarian type of building, again a Beaux-Art type of neoclassical design. But what is more intriguing is that it was built with the ability to conjure ethereal energy similar to what Tesla postulated his electromagnetic tower would do as noted by the Dome Stupa pointing straight into the sky's ionosphere. The architects of this building knew more than your average architect. Although the sentinel building was merely a copycat, it was not built to create this energy, but it looks like it could. However, other types of buildings within San Francisco were made robust enough to conjure this energy, particularly the Catholic churches built in the 1700s, before World War 1. They all had large cathedrals, domes and stupas to channel the ethereal energy from thin air, store it in the basement, and distribute it when needed.

Who were the builders of all these gothic Catholic churches before the 1900s? The Spanish Catholic churches wanted to monetize the free electrical energy to sell it to their very own constituents.

Tartarian stems back to King Solomon and the Tower of Babel. Geo, you are about to find out for yourself Geo. Your faith will lead you there.

Take your clothes off! Geo stops what he is doing and grins at Li. You cannot be serious, Li! I am very serious, Geo. Before entering that threshold, you must be fully naked, just you, Geo, nothing else but your body, thoughts, and soul, just like Adam. No clothes.

The monk starts the singing bowl, but this time without the honey bee, and starts ringing the bowl at a low to high pitch. As the Spectrum analyzer hits an inaudible frequency of 1.65ghz, the red doors automatically open. Beyond the doors, Geo can see purple-bluish fires within a dome. Geo is cautiously curious and walks closer.

Geo peers through the doors to see fire encircling this spherical room with walls 50-75 feet high and the flames burning like a fireplace around the structure. Glistening water flows from within massive Ionic columns with built-in waterfalls falling into aqua pools of water at the base of each fire encircling the dome. It is like a roman colosseum. The columns hold the huge elliptical dome ceiling like a large planetarium.

Geo is mesmerized. Every step he takes seems to take him into an ethereal, surreal path. Forgetting that he is naked, Geo is curious about this stunning dome.

Li instructs Geo to walk into the threshold of the doors and into the dome and sit in the middle of the floor. A masonry walk paves the way to the center of the coliseum. The atmosphere warm but neutral in temperature. Geo walks through the doors and follows the intricate inlaid brick paths to the center. Li's voice echoes through the doors as they close behind

him. Geo looks to the center of the dome and sees what appears to be a lit floating orb with rings on each axis that have lenses attached.

CHAPTER 17

TARTARIAN DOME OF MYRIAD

The Dome reached 100-200 and the inner diameter was an exact 72.20 feet in diameter with a deep ceiling crown extending to what looked like into the sky. The Dome ceiling was deceptive and underground about 250 feet. As the red doors sealed themselves, the unusual Orbs floated to guard anyone from entering or prying open the doors as "they" were guarding the entrance from anyone entering. The orbs were made of what looked like iron, yet had no propulsion system and somehow defied gravity. The many lenses wrapped on the orb's shiny glass rings rotated around the ring but looked like eyes with optical lenses that all focused independently. Geo was utterly lost in disbelief. The entire Dome and circular coliseum transitioned to what appeared to be a three-dimensional interactive hologram except in great, vivid 8k resolution and detail. The air within the room was crystal clear, like the air in the Antarctica ocean, and had a light, airy, clean feel. Geo could see precisely in high resolution, and his sense of smell and awareness became very keen. He could feel the goosebumps rising throughout his body, and his mental acuity was clearer than a GIA lab-grown diamond. The saturated colors within the Dome were vivid, and Geo stood up as the monk's singing bowl sound frequency became louder to a distinct southing pitch. A tiny orb suddenly appeared floating 40 feet from him, developing into a larger circular, spinning, spiral portal, and then suddenly standing in the middle, everything in the Dome flipped, and in a flash, everything became a large natural 360-degree open grassy field with trees, golden and green colored tall grass, shrubs, and hillsides in the background as if there were very real and colorful as Geo could see the orange-greenish colors of the leaves on the trees and the ants crawling in crooked linear formation up the tree bark to the leaky sap on a branch. There were glistening lakes and ponds to the farthest part of the fields and to the back of Geo, as the depth of the objects within the interactive hologram were all proportional and life-size. The upper Dome resembles the crystal-clear blue skies with broken alto-stratospheric clouds to the farther parts of the sky.

A sudden ease came over Geo. The Dome had become alive. A trusting atmosphere settled in as Geo could see some movement from afar. As Geo peered deep into the forest, he saw a fury four-legged creature approaching him from afar. It got closer and closer to Geo. It was a muscular, pearly white, luminous lion with a plush masculine mane, teeth like golden daggers, and paws far larger than Geo's naked feet. Fear instantly struck Geo as he looked to the orbs for guidance, and somehow, the orb's rings spun and locked into place, with all lenses focused on Geo. Somehow, it made Geo feel safe, although cautious at the tall 5-foot ominous-looking lion approaching him. The lion fiercely roared to show his respect to Geo as he merely passed by to observe and smell Geo as he walked off slowly and disappeared into the landscape.

Geo looked forward again and saw a strange-looking pride of pearly white luminous buffalos with thick manes and silverish long sharp horns, kicking up dust as they rumbled through the far landscape.

The pride turned to stampede in Geo's direction as the ground and trees shook violently. Geo stood frozen, and his body began to shake. The entire Dome shook as if it was an earthquake. The power of the white wildebeest stampeding towards Geo made him lower his stance and staunchly grip the bricks with his toes and bare feet.

There was nowhere to run. As the pride rushed towards Geo head-on, suddenly, they split their path to curve around Geo. The herd of hundreds stampeded around Geo to follow the luminous lion, and the pride disappeared too into the landscape, leaving dust blanketed everywhere like a thick fog. Geo could smell the damp, earthy humidity in the clay dirt as it flicked from the beasts' hooves into the air as they rushed by.

An alluring, luminous woman with long, flaxen hair and glowing pearly skin appeared like a ghost from the dust left behind. She stood seductively a semi-truck length away from Geo. Her larger-than-normal blue eyes were wide and hypnotic, and her mouth, framed with succulent lips, was small. She looked perfect by all standards. Too perfect to be human.

The sky turned dark as thunder and lightning began to swirl the atmospheric air in the mountains at the furthest part of the Dome.

Without a word, she approached Geo and stopped an arm-length away. She raised her arm and touched Geo's forehead with her shimmering index finger as Geo heard a voice within his head telepathically.

The Entity says, "You have not made a choice. You still have a choice, Geo!" Curious, Geo responds out loud, "Who are you? In the most supple, high-fidelity voice he had ever heard, the Entity purrs, "My name is Myriad. Do not fear. We will not hurt you. I cannot control you unless you allow me to. Just know you are here for a reason. There is nothing we do not know about you.

Geo grins, "We? You are not invited into my mind!"

Myriad explains, "This is how we communicate. In our domain, there is no other way. Welcome. "WE" are they and them, WE are many, and US is them."

Geo asks, "So, do you live here?" Myriad smiles and says, "We live here, there, everywhere: in the hot desert, in the cold ice, on the moon, in the stars, in the caves, in the air, in the oceans, below and above the firmament. We dwell in everything the ominous Endless created." Geo, "Endless?"

Myriad responds, "The Merciful Creator of Everything Infinite, Creator of Humans, and all living beings on earth and in heaven, me, WE, and yes, you too, Geo."

Geo says, "You are beautiful. Are you an Angel?"

Myriad smiles deceptively. "Indeed, we are angelic. The

Great Illuminated is our prince. We are wise and perfect on earth and here to watch humans. Geo asks, "Are you fallen?" Myriad blue eyes grow wide. "Yes, indeed we are."

Geo asks, "Are you a demon?" Myriad says, "No, but our half-human breed of deceased children are spirits that mutate into all living demons that take many forms in the space-time continuum. You have met some of them in the past. Myriad compels Geo's mind to remember a horrible experience he had as a child.

Geo sees the memory flash in his mind like a camera, filling him with fear, terror, and regret. "I was just a child! They tricked me into doing it. It was not my idea! I was a little boy, merely 5 years old, and like a fool, I agreed. I didn't know what I was doing! They took something from me!

Myriad says, "Yes, Geo, this is what our demons do best. But judging you here and now is not my place or duty. Today, our rabble, our legions, are manipulating humans every step of the way in your life. Creating impossible situations with impossible outcomes, never knowing what hits them or why. Yet you still made that choice and agreed. You always made bad choices, Geo, just like everyone else." Myriad's smile turns wicked as she giggles deeply. "Humans make it so easy for us. They are entertained by every evil coincidence since the Canaanites, mixed with our favorite demons of Jared's tribe. They taught the Canaanites every diversionary pursuit contrary to worship and homage to the Omnipotent Endless.

Today, Humans are too busy and distracted with their tiny technology, their tiny smartphones, and Canaanitic–Satanic sourced entertainment, sucking them dry until their spiritual energy evaporates. They are left with no spiritual energy field for Endless. Everything Humans touch today is quintessential satanic in its most natural form, so they all agree to it anyway and have no idea why. Just like you did when you were 5 years old, Geo."

Geo shouts, "They took something from me!"

Myriad scowls, "Being naive and ignorant of Endless's

truths is no excuse! We have no mercy towards women and men. There is no way out of your life choices, Geo, yet as a child, Endless forgives. But it doesn't keep our multitudes, WE, from training humans into our ways, so they willingly choose to hand over their souls directly or indirectly. We set the stage for impossibility. The odds are stacked against you. Don't blame us! We didn't make the rules. We just lead you in the direction to break them. For us, it's a game. We steal souls.

Things were much more transparent in the past. Human tribes would accept our demons as part of their lives equally with Endless's and his arch angels. It was black or white. One merely made a choice and learned to exist with the two options but never denied their existence. People choose Endless or Lucifer the Illuminated! Humans made a choice on their own. We weaved in and out of human lives. All colors and cultures of the world would sacrifice even their young to us in our allegiance to defy Endless. In exchange, over generations, we built the eloquent modern temples they desired. Few Humans understand this soul exchange; it's easier to mislead humans today. We start working on them as children until they are of age to make their own Godly and Ungodly choices. But Endless forgives the errors of children. But, as adults, Endless is horrendous in showing mercy.

Endless loved King David; therefore, the stakes were high for us to steal Solomon's Soul. The soul exchange was a value proposition with King Solomon. We agreed to build King Solomon's Temple. Even by today's standards, his Temple, as an homage to Endless, was the most advanced structure and technology in the world. We use the same dimensional formulas today to build our personal domains.

Our Battalions have hidden these truths and bought our way into human souls for pennies on the dollar. We even give 24k rods of gold in trade for their souls. Every form of our architecture follows the golden rules we created in building magnificent buildings to stand forever and ever. Marvel at this Dome Geo! We built this Dome thousands of years ago in the astrological era of Cancer. We enticed Solomon's unjustness and his sexual prowess and used it against him until he was kneeling before our deities. Our demonic army lifted those megalithic stones and pilasters to build his Godly temple, as we did in Turkey, Iran, Gaza, Azteca, and other parts of the world. No mass of humans could build what we did.

But Solomon sacrificed to our beloved Molech, who sacrificed children, in the same fashion people sacrifice themselves into fire at your burning man festivals and your televised satanic football and sports games. And how Hollywood movie stars and artists fancy sacrificing humans and children for their adrenochrome while you buy the notion that all this is merely entertainment. Some Hollywood stars and singers sacrifice their children for stardom.

We seal the deal with contracts: heart, mind, wallet, and soul! All in the name of Molech and our beloved Lucifer. Endless stepped away from Solomon's inadequacies and left him because he worshipped Molech and other deities and icons. In the end, we spite Endless by taking King David's Son to hell for the price of our hard labor.

We did the same with Nimrod's Tower of Babble. Our demon regimens were the first Masons who created the technology of bricks and megalithic architectural stones. Now the Free Mason and the Illuminati represent us via certain bloodline families pent up in Vatican City supported by IMF financial banking cartels in London and the armed forces and militia power of Washington DC, "The Tristate." Each tristate country incorporated an obelisk statue to confirm their allegiance to each other in controlling the masses of people worldwide for the past 2000 years. It is where the bloodline families rotate their positions and work with our demons in 500-year cycles.

The Vatican controls the people's spirituality. The City of London is where they finance the control. The inept Washington DC power military forces corrupt Democrat and Republican Congressmen. The Senators enforce worldly control through

NATO, the UN, and satanist corrupt politicians, judges, district attorneys, the FBI, CIA and government agency leadership. All of the ones who worship our demons and burn alms to our Molech Owl at the Boho grove and in their mansions at night.

"Our battalions returned to existing as spirits when we reached the optimum defilement of humans, and Endless threatened to flood our world. We built those pyramids long before Adam and Eve were created. Your historians have been hiding this truth for thousands of years and consistently lie about history to keep our reality secret. Endless and Lucifer appear to be a fictional paradigm in your perception of reality today, but they are real and before you.

The Egyptians discovered and inhabited our architecture as they began to repopulate the world again after the floods. We had abandoned them during this worldly destruction of humans the first time Endless flexed his anger. Thousands of years later, the Egyptian pharaohs delivered their souls to us in our temples and spires, worshipping us in our original abodes. We inaugurated these human dynasties for 3000 years into our deception, Pharoah after Pharoah. Our lands, properties, and great cities all over the planet, including the Chin Dynasty and Dynasties before Chin existed long before Endless created Adam. Our demons are hardworking and industrious. How could we not be when Endless created us."

Geo asks, "Are you saying you built the Pyramids in Gaza? "Yes, many thousands of years before the Pharaohs arrived. We have fallen long ago and roamed the earth before the Garden.

We worship in the cities we built for ourselves and for the Great Illuminated, yet we have a longer relationship with Endless than humans. But we remain in defiance; we ask Endless for forgiveness as Heaven falls more closely within our refined taste a bit better than does our stay here on earth. We fear Endless. Endless never recants a promise, and we are confined here until Endless's prophecies are fulfilled. You and We are part of that fulfillment.

Before and even now, the Archangels imprisoned us and

held some of us hostage to frustrate us. So, we hide and corrupt humans any chance we get in the most insidious ways to enlighten our Great Illuminated for the time being. That is why we hide here in this Dome. The local Chinese people constantly pop traditional fireworks, causing noise, distraction, and confusion, keeping the archangels guessing where we hide underground."

The video reels keep playing every word Myriad utters inside the Dome as Geo sees how Myriad and her demons manipulated dominated the world since their arrival.

"When humans came into existence, we found it more beneficial and lucrative for us to spite Endless by stealing souls, and we devised many ways of doing so even this very minute.

But without a soul to conjure our governance over them, there would be no reason to build any more buildings. We taught humans the knowledge of iron and metal, science and math, technology and construction, all for the price of their souls. From astrological-to-astrological age, we built and destroyed in our defiance of Endless until today. The Astrological age is soon changing again as we are headed for Aquarius, and things are about to change in a very big way, Geo! Human souls are valuable bargaining chips for us when negotiating what you call technology but what is merely natural to us. The more value souls bring, the more we offer. In the end, we won because our grand leader, the Illuminated, controls all elements, even the atomic elements that build this world.

As you can see by all of the archeological remnants and artifacts of lost civilization after lost civilization, eon after eon, century after century, we won with the destruction of humanity, and what they perceived as a utopian culture here on earth is merely lies that we fed to the leaders to reach all humans through their forms of propaganda. We repeat the process over and over until nothing, but remnants and artifacts are left. All you find are cities underwater and deep in the earth. Then, the next generation of leaders hides this real past, so the next crop of humans knows no difference between their authentic value and the altruistic value of Endless." Myriad starts laughing out loud!

Geo asks, "There is no heaven on earth?"

Myriad says, "There is no Utopia on Earth. There is only Heaven, as Heaven was created by Endless. You are all slaves to yourselves here on earth. We let you destroy yourselves. You all agreed to enslave yourselves in one form or another. We just provide Humans with the hierarchal structures to do so until you obliterate yourselves by your own will.

We are very unique and powerful on this earth. We can fly. In fact, our flying is much more complex than what you can imagine, but we don't need riveted wings of aluminum or jet fuel turbine engines, and we telepathically communicate without the need or use of insubstantial smartphones, and our technology does not short circuit, rust or break. We are forever and live forever under our Endless wrath and holy laws. We are different than you, although WE admire you.

Geo wrinkles his brow, "You admire me?" Myriad says, "Of course, like Adam, you and WE are beautiful creatures. We present ourselves to man as Gods/Goddesses with fine, immaculate taste. Still, humans perceive us, as Hollywood perceives us, as ugly and scary beings, ghosts, aliens, reptilians, Skinwalkers, bigfoots, zombies, gnomes, elves, werewolves, Chupacabra, etc. Humans create these evil images and contrive stories to deceive themselves and put themselves in constant fear, to deluge and distract themselves from having faith and concentration on Endless. Even your concept of Lucifer is silly and worthy of being put in a bottle of Louisiana Red Devil Hot sauce. Humans have limited creativity, and when their minds cannot determine an object, their minds extrapolate from their memory cells and configure all sorts of mental adaptations far from their concept of reality and the truth to substantiate their belief structures and not veer far from their mental capacities to feel secure. So "Myriad" obliges them and enhances their perception of reality to deceive them into submitting their souls to US no matter what they believe US to be. Although we take different forms worldwide, WE are One and one of many, and we are born to deceive humans in their state of thinking and their concepts of reality.

Humans believe there is a matrix of sorts, but it is merely the propaganda they have accepted since childhood. There is only one reality, and because humans live in their own made-up matrices, they believe everything else above their contextual mindsets is a matrix. Humans are the matrix, not US. It is easy to deceive Humans within their complex made-up mental matrices."

Geo asks, "Are you saying little Grey Men are our own fabrication?"

Myriad responds, "Yes. You perceive them as either gnomes, reptilians, or aliens from inner earth or outer space. The caricatures are merely your fabrication within your own matrix. FYI Denys (James) Watkins-Pitchford, a human, created this concept. Instead of accepting the truth about who we realistically are, you believe written fabrications from authors, historians, and the hoax media and accept them truer than any truth you have ever discovered on your own.

You fabricate everything to appear delusional other than the authentic US as physically beautiful, angelic, and demonic creatures.

Because the instant you accept the notion of US, of Myriad, and the Great Illuminator is the very instant that you must acknowledge the notion of Endless, AN INEFFABLE GOD!

You distract yourselves from the knowledge and faith in Endless. You are pleasantly stuck in the small riches and quaint lives we negotiated for you that you accept. So, you believe we can only come to humans in clunky shitty lenticular spaceships from some scientific Orwellian science-fiction novels.

Do you remember your crazy Uncle Biggs?"

Geo squints, "Biggs? I never thought he was crazy. He was a good person. I remember the stories of his abductions and UFO encounters he would tell the family when we were camping. We believed in him, but not necessarily his stories. Did you mess with Biggs? He committed suicide, you know. They found his corpse off the beach in Sausalito; the high tide brought him to shore, his body broken to pieces after jumping off the Golden Gate. He was a good guy. A Vietnam Viet who saw a lot of acts of war."

Myriad smiles, "Yes, Good ole Biggs. Imagine publicly telling everyone you saw a green alien, never imagining the ridicule you would receive from your people, your society. Times are changing today. You see little green aliens because they cannot hide any longer. Your leaders cannot hide the truth from you, either. But you only see the construct of an alien you were programmed to see, i.e., little green men. It is WE in disguise.

Your powerful governmental ministry of disinformation keeps Humans all twisted in thought. The same agency that is supposed to be truthful to the public and debunk fallacies and propaganda is programming you to rival the same truths. Twisted! They keep you in suspended disbelief and keep your pineal gland open just enough so that WE can fit right into it. That is what we did to your Good Ole Biggs until he chose to end it all with a leap of faith straight into the ocean. Cha-ching!"

Geo screams at Myriad, "Biggs was a good uncle! I am done with hating evil things. As much as I want to loathe you, I understand that I don't like what I see here."

Geo reminds himself that calmer minds prevail, so he decides to merely listen and ask questions, as this is his golden opportunity to understand the essence of his existence and the reality of the world.

Myriad continues, "It would be easier for humans to have faith in Endless rather than you figure out billions of ways to work around Endless even at the risk of your integrity and logic as souls.

We negotiate only with the best of Kings, Leaders, and purest of souls of this world. We defile all others with no negotiating power or value to US, representing 99% of all humans. Valueless, competitive, egotistical beings are all easily corruptible, stuck in traffic and waiting in lines. All easily mislead as yourself, Geo."

Geo calmly asks, "Are you saying that I have no value?"

Myriad explains, "We only give the value you give yourself, Geo. The more influence you have over people, the more value we give you. The more faith you have in Endless, the more valuable you are to US, and the larger the stakes in negotiating with us. If you want gold, stardom, castles, or a mansion, then you better have some form of value. Otherwise, you will end up drugged and addicted on some street corner infested with our armies and legions willing to take your cheap soul even at that useless rate. We love addicts. Addictions are an easy gateway into a person's body and soul. We scale that with the infiltration of more alcohol and drugs. Some of our most extraordinary statistics come from addictions.

The Mexican Cartels are scoring huge statistics for US in the United States. Especially now that there are no borders to your country, WE are spreading the cartels internationally. The US Secretary of Homeland Security, the border czar is a freemason in our pyramid structure. Our Legion is in Mayorkas's ears this very moment. He is under our control.

Geo asks, "Is that what those notarized contracts represent? They are signed with their blood and souls.

Myriad, "Now you are getting the picture, Geo. You are not the closer, but as a legal witness, you facilitate the contractual closing of a person's soul or the way to their soul in any part of that equation. You are being used, a pawn."

Geo, "I see. I am a conduit to reach far more than one soul here."

Myriad says, "Yes, it is like a chess game, Geo. You chose to play; you didn't have to play? But you wanted to pay your bills, right! You want to regain your past, right! You have always had a choice; as a 5-year-old child, you chose to be here. Sometimes, you occupy the black space for bad deeds and sometimes the white space for good deeds, for better or worse or worse for better. We play people against each other, war in and war out.

Ultimately, you knock each other out from pawn to pawn, bishop to bishop, queen to queen, and king to king. Ultimately, whatever good or bad you did doesn't really matter. It is an end game we designed. So far, history proves that Myriad is winning. The Great Illuminated is content."

Geo says, "You are a beautiful creature, and I see your value. Is this the way Endless created you?"

Myriad smiles, "Oh, you like? Of course, this is the real me. Lucifer is also beautiful, and his voice is supple, as are all in our battalions. We were all created by Endless.

Geo, "Are you a female?" Myriad winks, "No, I am Myriad. I am WE and US and THEM in my Legion." Geo asks, "Pronouns? Where have I heard this socialist, Marxist-inspired pronoun jargon before?" Myriad responds, "We are here to set identity confusion in adults and groom their children by creating many different identities and making your young susceptible to our enlightened sexuality and self-identities for the youth. We train them when they are young, so they accept us easily when they mature, sometimes in adolescence. It is easier for US to enter the youth when they are confused about their true physical and spiritual identity as boys and girls.

"It does not surprise me why people use these "pronouns agendas" these days. Strictly from the Illuminated, right!" As Geo says in a humorous tone under his breath, as if Myriad cannot hear his thoughts. He continues, "All those TV commercials and Netflix movies using predictive programming are being used on our youth today."

Myriad's words echo in the Dome. Each time Myriad speaks a pronoun, a movie of children being misled plays as a 3D hologram in the Dome.

Geo, "The Devil is in the Details, right?!!

As Myriad continues speaking about the history, every story is portrayed as a hologram in a 3D bubble on the walls, ceilings, and floors of the Dome. Images of the Sumerians, Pharaohs, the Chin Dynasty, Babylon to the Roman Empires, Mayans to the Inquisition.

Myriad's memory of the Lucifer's bataillon point-of-view, every story from Myriad's beautiful mind plays before Geo's eyes like a Hollywood movie within the Dome.

Frame by frame, like a precisely edited, professionally directed movie that plays on the big screen for Geo to watch, unlike any movie he had ever seen. In the skies of the Dome were all sorts of flying objects, countless UFOs, small and big orbs, ticktacks, bell-shaped, polarogram-shaped saucers whizzing through the sky. While in the Southern portion of the Dome, a lightning storm was brewing, yet the objects had no concern about the storm. While the movie plays to Myriad's soft, telepathic voice, Geo sees different creatures hiding in the trees in the far-off forest. Little green men, tall greys, strong reptilians, and a trio of three Nordics, all in the background playing hide and seek with Geo. Everything all at once, like a montage, spilled onto reality, and yet everything seemed serious and grim in its overall tone.

As the hologram continues, magnificent architectural buildings arise from the ground and collapse to create one after the other. First, the Tower of Babel, then King Solomon Temple, and all of the pyramids from the Pharaohs to the Mayans arose and were crushed to dust.

Next came the medieval gothic Neo-Classic and Tartarian buildings all around the world, one after the other before Geo's eyes as Myriad spoke. Myriad words were played in 360-degree 3D 8k resolution.

Myriad continues, "As time moved on after we thwarted the Roman Empire in 475AD, in succession, we taught the Indo-Europeans the value of our architecture and technology through Genghis Khan and his Mongolian children when they were ripe enough to know our secrets. We allowed him to conquer all of Asia, creating Tartaria. We taught Tatarians to build fabulous megalithic complexes, neo-classic cities, and star ports throughout Asia, China, Peking, India, Germania, Norway, Finlandia, Ireland, and Scotland. WE gave them much knowledge and armor to enslave and destroy each other as an experiment compared to chimps. With the skills that we gave them, they broke away from tribes to become better and bigger nations, eventually to their own demise, sweeping everyone six feet under.

Geo asks, "Breakaway civilizations? Are we a breakaway civilization?"

Myriad says, "Not anymore. You used to be, but not anymore. Only select bloodlines have been given the most up-to-date technologies to keep you in control until the right time. They are taking ownership of all technology by copyright, patents, and trademarks of all tech and reselling to you at 100x the value. These families keep you close like dogs on leashes; ironically, you seem to love it.

Tartaria was an intelligent breakaway race. Today, their bloodlines run actively and alive, breeding different strong subcultures. Even Hitler was fascinated with Ariosophy in creating his bastardized version of Aryans. Hitler is indirectly tied to the Council of 13. Even the Bushes supplied him with support and supplies. Does it surprise you that American companies were coconspirators against the Jews? It was just one of our other ploys. We took about 60 million total souls in WW2. How is that for success? Our Legions started working in parallel with the remaining Romans converted to Jesuits and Roman Catholics. This is where we decided to expand and redevelop North and South America and Europe as the ancient natives were becoming ripe in our worship in those parts."

The 3D movie continues to run.

Myriad, "We sought for more souls. In the name of the Holy Catholic Church, we conquered, via Columbus and Cortez, the entire continents. Before them, we gave Montezuma our old structures and civilizations, kingdoms and gold that he was willing to sacrifice his children even by having an appetite for them for, and then we swept them and his civilization off the bloody sacrificial table for a new team of Spanish Roman Catholic bandits who were more precise in killing and interested in populating the world faster than could ever be imagined.

The Roman Catholics had a very special skill in manipulating the masses. The "MASSES would have to be convinced that to be absolved of their sins, they would have to atone but only through confessions, even though fallible pontiffs are merely human and not omnipotent as communicating with merciful Endless directly.

These Roman Catholics were a stroke of genius of cunning manipulation and death machine bar none. The Roman Catholics cut Endless right out of his son's own church and handed it to us scripturally and methodically through the traditions they created. The masses have no idea who they worship at Sunday MASS and how we demonized these Popes through our legions. We sought and placed the most corruptible influential family bloodlines loyal to us that had strong bloodline genetics to the Canaanites. WE converged them into this pyramid, uniting a One World Order plan and dividing the power between these clandestine families. Thirteen families, to be exact.

The Council of 13 formed the 2nd to the top layer of the Pyramidion power structure that we see on the backside of the US dollar today. Thirteen stars represent the thirteen bloodlines that formed the 13 colonies in the New World. One colony per family as agreed and signed for in blood.

Geo asks, "You are referring to the Illuminati?" "Of course, Geo, they are as real as your US dollar. There are 13 iconic stars representing the council of 13 on that dollar; their favorite owl icon is hidden on that bill. The Illuminati families are the most valued human assets. They control the "Tristate" that I just mentioned! They control the world by departmentalization in layers within the pyramid structure."

Geo surmises, "So, 13 families control the world via Washington DC for war power, The Vatican for spiritual influence, and London for world financial power?" Myriad says, "Yes, we are coconspirators. The Tristate and the Council of 13 work alongside US within the Pyramidion as the Crowned Council of 13. Since Endless gives free choice, we are kept from influencing humans directly. Thus, we use the very influential Illuminati and their worldly control over people through religion, war, and money to bring humans to us, giving every individual the power to choose their destiny.

Geo asks, like an investigator, "Who are the families?

As Myriad exclaims "My lips are sealed". But some historic names shoot across the sky with their families of then and now all in one hologram "Bruce, De Medici, Cavendish, Hanover, Kennedy, Hapsburg, Plantagenet, Romanov, Sinclair, St. Clair, Windsor, Warburg, Krupp, Del Banco, Saxe-Coburg-Gothe, Rothchild, Bauer, Orsin, Pindar, Schiff, and Rockefeller as they have grown in population, a hundred thousand family members have this bloodline. Geo watches their faces appear one after the other as AI conceives this in the Dome. You may be aware of some of these historic figures. They are very much in action and have powers of control today like no other governmental structure, but that is for you to research and see who is who. My lips are sealed. The family members are tracked as preferred stock via their social security cards red

numerical code listed on back of the US social security card. All other people are considered common stock people. DNA ancestral test is designed to find preferred stock individual bloodline connection to the Council ancestral families and to associate and give them access to power and finances as the council family members need a trusted workforce.

For thousands of years, the Illuminati families have yielded successful results for US, and we have rewarded them gratefully. They go by many different last names, although DNA proves their bloodline. Each of their thousands of members is of great value to us, and you have met and signed some here in San Francisco. Do you remember the APEC conference that Xi Jinping attended? Well, you defiantly signed one of these bloodline members at the JW Marriot here who is running for a Californian senator seat in congress and who is at our dispense and whom we compromised through pedophilia. He is of the

Redshield family ancestry. Geo, "I remember that grifter trying to take our 45th president down through impeachment". His hands were nervous and shaky when he signed his contract. I despised that signing, but I was professional. Myriad, "Not to worry we will deal with him as we own his soul and will discard him soon"

Geo asks, "So, all the bad and evil in this world is caused by people and not you? "If you recall, Geo, humans choose. They have free will to negotiate with us or not. Even though we are insidious, we absolutely abide by Endless's rules. Endless was very clear with Lucifer the Great Illuminated when he was ejected from heaven, and he abides by the rules the Great Creator Endless has put forth.

Geo says, "Ah, I see now clearly. The Illuminati is correlated to Lucifer, the Great "Illuminated." This is who has been signing documents?

Myriad says, "Yes, Geo, the Council of 13 sign their names in blood to our contracts and whom they contract with. When it is written, it shall be done. You have witnessed it all. We need proof for Endless so his archangels do not frustrate or audit our intentions. You are our commissioned witness with evidence, and we have rewarded you with much cryptocurrency.

Geo nervously says, "Oh, I was just doing my job. So, you were there? Were you at Khris Larsin's home with me? Myriad says, "Yes, I observed your reconnaissance skills to become wealthy in digital assets. That is why Khris's dog Joel pissed all over your foot."

As Myriad spoke, a surveillance video from Khris Larsin's home on Larsen Street replayed and showed Geo glancing at some documents that fell out of a folder on his dining room table. It turns out that Khris was transferring millions of dollars' worth of the XRPP token, depleting the supply and making the value soar of that crypto token.

Myriad says, "Insider trading pays off, Geo. Just ask House Representative Pelosi if it pays. Laughing $400 million rich on a House Representative's meager pay? We got her number. Geo, "It is alleged that she is the daughter and wife of a Freemason." Geo defends himself, "There is no rule against insider trading in the crypto world, as the XRPP token is not a security." I couldn't help reading what was before me as I was merely glancing at the areas to be notarized on that financial transfer order form. So, you cannot blame me."

Myriad scowls, "But ironically, later that evening you deposited your entire savings into the crypto exchange and bought 100,000s of tokens for pennies, right before the token soared and made you millions, right?'

Geo says, "You cannot prove anything."

"You're right, Geo, we have no proof. Yet that is not the point here. When Khris's dog pissed on your foot, you stood up in surprise and accidentally flipped open the folder. You see, we can command animals too. I was in that room too. Even his puppy Joel, was rewarded for pissing on your foot when we gave you this crypto and golden opportunity. Khris Larsin is one of our devotees and a World Economic Socialist Forum (WESF) member, not to mention a CIA informant who is part of the Tristate. Don't worry; his crypto corporation did very well on that transfer, and the Illuminati has plans for that organization when everything gets monetized in digital currency to control the masses more precisely.

Suppose, Geo, that we control your ability to spend currency digitally. In that case, we will eventually dominate you easily. Your society is headed in that direction with crypto and your help. Do you understand how we work now?"

Geo says, "Yes. I take full responsibility for my actions."

Myriad laughs, "What actions Geo? Consider it water under the bridge. We needed a human with integrity and a weakness to witness for us."

Geo says, "My daughter is my only weakness. I would do anything for her." "Ah, Geo, Summer, we know all of your weaknesses."

A memory video starts playing in the Dome. Everything

else ceases. All creatures and objects stop to see this video as Geo cradles Summer in his arms. Her long copper hair sways softly like a Lilypad in the water as the sunlight glistens on Summer's face as he walks her around the swimming pool, humming to Summer as she falls asleep to the rhythm of the waterfall.

Geo says softly, "That was a beautiful time of my life. I miss it tremendously. Thank you for that memory. Have I inadvertently sold my soul to you?"

Myriad almost emphasizes, "Not yet. You still have yet to make a choice with Endless, but your time is arriving, and the future could be clearer, to be perfectly honest with you. But our bets are on you. By all the billions of human interactions we manipulate, great and small, we capsize civilizations. Yet before we do, we keep those spiritual contracts on file and their signatures notarized in their blood. That is how we prove their bloodline. Our organizational skills have no bounds. We tend to get valuable humans on record even if they do not sign by blood. The others agree implicitly by saying nothing and going with the flow of things, just like you did with the crypto. We just tossed in a tip for you as a thank you."

Geo shrugs, "I bagged a few million on that trade and invested the rest in gold. Myriad smiles, " I know. Gold is a classy move, Geo!

Every 500 years, the Illuminati rotate power positions within the Vatican, Washington DC, and The City of London, with the leading family addressing how they will populate the world to deliver souls.

Ors is the gray pope. The most shadowy figure that no Catholic ever realized. He is the 13th bloodline from Maxima's and Claudia's clans. There are 13 familial Popes, 125 Cardinals, and endless senators representing massive territory. Ors controls the black and white Popes. He is the most powerful man, bar none. He chairs the Council of 13 as the honorable rat towering over the land of Scaven, manipulating and officiating under the unique guise of the other 12 members. He resides in the Vatican and controls the military of 125 countries, hospitals, the Secret Service, paramedic services, the FBI via Homeland Security, CIA, CDC, NIH, UN, WHO, FEMA, WHO, Red Cross, etc., etc., etc.

The Hologram video shows Ors's handsome cavalier face and appearance turns demonic.

He is quite the charmer in governing the Popes. We call him the "Grey Pope," the leader, and to his left, the "Black Pope," Superior General of the Order of Jesuits, Arcturus Soza. He is our little socialist controller. "Black Pope" refers to the fact that, unlike the Pope, who wears white, the Superior General, an ordinary high priest, wears black. The Jesuits are referred to as a powerful force within the Catholic church. Under Ors, the Grey Pope is a powerful individual in the Church, arguably one of the most powerful, despite not being a cardinal or bishop. As the head of the Jesuit order, the Superior General makes a special vow of loyalty to the Pope. We gave Arcturus the power of telepathy to control his worshipers. The actual Pope is the "White Pope, "the bishop of Rome, currently Pope Panchito.

Like the chess board or the same Masonic checkered floor, you see in Oddfellow temples or its derivative sites, they are all layers within the structure under the Pyramid. They use the checkerboard to posture their position within the Pyramid and allegiance to the Popes and bloodline families infested with our demons within the Pyramidion.

The Black Pope creates deviant insidious activities worldwide and creates and controls corrupt governments, agencies, leaders, politicians, militaries, corporations, and NGOs. And the White Pope is in charge of all the good that happens within world governments, contradicting every step that the Black Pope moves, tit for tat. The Grey Pope, the front, is kind and evil at the same time and monetizes the Catholic Church via the Tristate I mentioned earlier. The Tristate is the Pyramid in its totality.

There wouldn't be any way to monetize strictly doing good or evil independently. If everyone was evil, there would be no hope or faith to do anything. So, the White Pope brings hope, the Black Pope brings decay and destruction to all the efforts of the White Pope and his supporters. And, of course, there is no Utopia on Earth, so the White pope is futile. The Tristate is a well-choreographed dance, a circus and a Banana republic of sorts at our control.

Ors rings in the wealth and the spoils of the world, and more souls delivered to Myriad, so I may account this to my Lucifer the Great Illuminator."

The Movie of the Popes continues to play in the Dome.

Every 500 years, a new family of Council of 13 fights to be in the Grey Pope's controlling position, and we are nearing the end of that in the perceived Gregorian year with an entire zodiac cycle of 25,722 years.

Geo is surprised, "You mean the Age of Aquarius is coming? Myriad informs, "It began in 2012. The Mayans had precise calendars. They were right. While the world expected something different in 2012, they will start to see it in 2030 on your calendar.

Myriad holds court, saying, "In these past 500 years, you have witnessed a golden period of growth and enlightenment, but now, this new age will usher in one of pure darkness for the world and its people that even Vlad the Impaler would marvel at. Can you understand what the Tristate has been up to at the behest of Myriad and Ors in the Pyramidion?

Geo asks, "So, there is a real Lucifer?" Myriad says, "Yes, as real as you and I." "Myriad, so then Endless, God, is real?" "Yes, Geo, that is absolute."

The movie stops, lighting and thunder roars in the Dome.

Geo shutters, "Are you going to take my soul now?"

Myriad shouts, "No! Not now. Do you understand who and why you are here? Are you listening? Endless created this world, Myriad and Lucifer only operate in this world within the Tristate, and who controls the Tristate?

Geo shakes his head, "Yes. Now, it is very apparent. Thank you. "Very Good Geo! So, you believe in Myriad." "Yes, I do believe in Myriad & Lucifer! So, what am I here for?"

Myriad says with zeal, "Good, Very, very good. The year 2030 approaches."

Geo asks, "Are you referring to the agenda 2030 established by the United Nations and pushed by WESF and other NGOs and governments? Myriad says, "Yes", The Tristate in its totality is created. WE are pushing now, a one-world government, as we are at the beginning of the Age of Aquarius. The New World Order."

The Hologram starts playing with the Mayan pyramids and priests.

"Let me explain, Geo. The Mayans would have celebrated the end of their great cycle of 5,126 years on their calendar, which would have happened on our Gregorian calendar of 2012 if Mayans and the Aztecs were still alive and marked the conclusion of a bák'tun a time period in the Mesoamerican Long Count calendar.

Although many people believe that 2012 was marking the Doomsday of the Mayans and the world as we knew it, the truth is The Spanish Inquisition, dictated by the bloodlines and Cortez, amongst other Spanish Generals, eliminated the Aztec and Mayan empires 800-900 years ago, 2012 was definitely not the end of their world or the world as their empires were destroyed and left into jungle ruins in 1400-1600 AD centuries. There was a big "Nothing Burger" that happened in 2012 in North or South America or the world in 2012, although many suspected that the world would, in fact, come to an end. As much as I would have enjoyed an early doomsday, obviously, WE are still here. Nothing happened!

But the Mayan calendar predicted correctly that the actual year was merely a reference point in the Zodiac astrological age of change and ushering in the Age of Aquarius. We are moving into a new 2,160-year astrological age cycle of disastrous change for humans. The Dark Ages appear before humans again, Geo, and we have an agenda.

It is time for Ors and the Red Bears and Red Shields bloodlines to give up their 500-year reign power position with the Council of 13 as the Gray Popes and as agreed by the Council with their names written in our contract in blood. A new family will rule the Black and White Pope seats, too. Ors is becoming rather effective in handling business and wealth, driven by his greed, but has become rather inefficient at conjuring death. He has become soft! He forgot his agreement with US. He, amongst the Tristate, are all talk now and very little action. The bald-headed bumbling idiot at the WESF, reminds me of Dr. Evil from the silly Austin Powers movie. That grifter! We arm his father and family with nuclear weapons, and all they do is bring the world a fancy little flu crown snake venom virus and a RMNA graphene vaccine with only a mere 15 million Covid deaths worldwide over three long years of wasted time. We are running out of time, Geo! This world does not need weak, Dr. Fauci's, but we need more Josef Mengele's at the helm! Your population has grown to over 8 billion humans in this world. We need more souls! Our Great Illuminator is getting antsy, waiting for Ors's empty promises to be fulfilled. Ors shows some activity. Some minor uprisings in Myanmar, famine in Africa, Venezuela, Haiti, Yemen, a war here and there, some civil disobediences and fentanyl deaths in the US and a few beheadings in Mexico, A war between Ukraine and Russia with only 500,000 deceased Ukrainian soldiers is nothing but a drop in the bucket of US. While disrespecting us with a Joey-Bag-O-Donuts crackhead president's son. Ors's failed promises is wearing Myriad's patience thin!! Myriad wants WW3!! Lucifer wants WW3. WE WANT WW3."

As Myriad's voice turns duplicitously demonic, the entire Dome lit up.

Geo asks, "WW3?" "Yes!" Myriad arms fly out, showing an illuminant naked, voluptuous, tall body with brilliant blue flames shooting from Myriad's palms to the Dome's sky. Myriad's skin tone and eyes turn to an orange-red hue like the sun burning hydrogen.

The Dome lights up in fiery flames as "WW3" spews from Myriad's mind telepathically and spreads throughout the Dome. After a few minutes, the Dome becomes a grassy field again, and Myriad regains her pearly white color, deep blue eyes, and calm composure.

Geo asks, "What is the wait then?" Myriad says, "FRAMEWORK X!" Geo is perplexed, "FRAMEWORK X?"

Myriad calmly says, "Ors is claiming a "defect" in his blood-signed and notarized contract with US. He claims the year his ancestor bloodline signed the blood contract differed from the current actual chronological day, month, and year and that the timeline in history are all in error. Ors is claiming a void contract based on this defect. His greed binds him to this contractual defect and voids the performance of his bloodline contract with US.

Ors has been working alongside what mainstream historians call a "pseudohistorical conspiracy theorist" Dimitri Anatole Fominski, a Russian statistician/aerospace engineering professor. All the leading historians and archeologists claim Dimitri Anatole is a pseudoscientist without merit. Although Dimitri Anatole has done his homework and research precisely and discovered several significant facts about how the Jesuits created mainstream timeline chronologies here.

The Jesuits and Roman Catholics were in error. A truth that cannot go unaccountable to the archangels as something as significant as WW3 needs absolute proof. WW3 is the war to end all wars on Earth. If we want to usher in Agenda 2030 and the Age of Aquarius, we require full transparency to Endless. Lucifer will not tolerate insolence from the US, and Endless will not allow us to move forward regardless of the zodiac age transition without absolute proof. A signed contract and commitment of bloodlines make a firm concrete agreement of their allegiance with Lucifer. Free-choice remember! Our Fallen can only start the process by fully performing our angelic duty and proving contracts to the archangels.

Dimitri Anatole claims that today is not 2023. He claims that historians were all wrong as Sir Isaac Newton had grave problems with his lunar and solar eclipse tables and mechanical and mathematical issues with leap years. Dimitri Anatole claims that the Jesuits and Catholics used Newton's eclipse tables, and are chronologically incorrect. He says Jesuits fabricated bits and pieces of history, even art, to benefit their Roman Catholic rule over the world.

FRAMEWORK X

Dimitri Anatole has studied Sir Isaac Newton's eclipse tables and found very serious issues with how Newton calculated and introduced fabricated forces to account for lunar inconsistent forces which caused erratic accelerations and decelerations of the moon around the earth and incorporated these errors within lunar eclipse tables which historians and Jesuits later relied upon. Other notable historic mathematicians as Russian mathematician Anatoly Timofeevich Fomenko and prior mathematicians also had enhanced accurate and complete research regarding Sir Isaac Newtons fallacious eclipse tables. Newton's erroneous lunar tables were later used by the Jesuits, Catholics and historians to account for a falsified history and timeline itself into world calendars. These tables were used by the Jesuits in the 1600's to create erroneous and fallacious calendars which are used by the world today. Newton and the Jesuits all knew that Newton's errors were factual, but played in favor to control the history of time placing all events of history in a fabricated order for absolute control and into the pyramid structure of for the council of 13. If you control history then you control perception and thought.

A hologram movie plays, showing Dimitri's Dimitri Anatole working alone on mathematical equations on a board in his classroom.

Geo smiles, So, "Winston Churchill was right when he said "history is written by the victors"?

Myriad responds, "Napoléon called it *"A Fable Agreed Upon"*. Dimitri Anatole is in Ors's ear, and Ors has us by our luminescent balls. We need to change this immediately!

Geo, we want to sign a contract with Dimitri Anatole. We will give him wealth, mansions, cars, women, everything if he will recant any truth to his chronological mathematics of time. We want to buy him his brand and research out copyrights and all. We have set up an all-expense paid trip for Dimitri Anatole to travel to San Francisco for a CMNN newscast interview with him at The Marquis Hotel as a front. There will be beautiful women there for him to seduce him after the interview. Satriana, our best contract closer temptress in the world, will offer him great success if he signs our contract in blood. She is perfect in every way. Dimitri Anatole will fall in love with her. If we can get Dimitri Anatole to rescind and disavow his chronological findings and change his dissertations with Ors, then Ors's void claim is resolved. Ors could not pose a legal argument or claim a defect in contract Then, WE will move forth according to Lucifer's future timeline.

Geo asks, "You will appear there on time dressed to impress and to notarize Dimitri Anatole?" "Yes, in return, Geo, I will grant you all your wishes forever, and you will outlive everyone in this world with your daughter, Summer, beside you, even though WW3. We have prepared a safe and beautiful tropical island for you and your family to live out your legacy comfortably for the rest of your lives.

Do you believe in me, Geo?" "YES, I DO, MYRIAD!"

Satisfied, Myriad smiles, "Until we meet again, Geo."

Myriad walks back towards where she came from. Loud thunder erupts as rain starts pouring from the far-off forest. Geo sees the white lion roar into ominous clouds, shaking the Dome's core. As Geo finds his balance, the orbs retracted into the sky and faded. The Red Teutonic doors slowly open on their own. As the rain pummels down hard, Geo sprints out the doors as fast as he can to be released from the Dome. A magnetic force drops Geo onto the Dojo mat as he passes through the threshold.

Lyu, Li's, fierce Win Chung warrior stands there awaiting him.

CHAPTER 18

LYU THE MIGHTY WARRIOR

Geo lays nude on the soft bamboo knit mat where he landed fleeing the Dome. He is in deep recovery, sleeping for hours. Lyu covered Geo in a wool blanket and pillow under his head as he slept under the foggy San Francisco haze, peering in through the skylight. Lyu, nicknamed Aguila, "Eagle," is Li's most valuable mighty warrior. She is fast and empowered with keen eyesight, especially at night.

Lyu sits still, mindfully waiting for Geo to wake. In her meditation, she longed for her parents and younger brother in Mexico as it once was. Although she was born in Chile, her family migrated as immigrants to Mexico to farm avocado orchards. A crop that had risen in great value over all other crops. Her father, Gabriel, a Brazilian, was an ambitious, hardworking local farmer who used to be a businessman but saw Argentina becoming fundamentally socialistic and brought his family to Mexico for a better place with his wife, Candelaria Maria, to raise Lyu and her young brother Salvador.

In her lucid dream, Lyu briskly straggled as fast as any 12-year-old schoolgirl could from her school through the warm tropical forest and avocado field next to her home. She was running for her life when she learned from another student a cartel gang was holding her family hostage. Her worn school boots were ripe with green creamy avocados that had fallen to the ground. As she trampled them in haste, they stuck to her boot treads, causing her to slip on the moist earth as she ran into her farm orchards. The Aztecs pronounced avocados "ahuacatl," meaning testicle. The Aztecs were very practical at naming their fruits. To the ancients, Ahuacatl was a superfood that would naturally increase testosterone levels in people, explaining Lyu's strong determination, inner strength, and resilience to what was before her. She loved eating avocados on warm, freshly made French bread with salt and pepper.

As Lyu finally reached her farm's perimeter, three new, dusty G-5 Mercedes Benz parked on the front lot. Gabriel, her father, was kneeling on the front lawn with his face buried in his knees. A group of sun-browned, sweaty, macho Mexican men wearing black cowboy hats, pointy snakeskin Tony Lama boots, camouflage shirts, and jeans were loitering around toting AK47s and rooting for their compadre gang leader, EL Toro, to put a bullet through Gabriel's forehead. El Toro held the 24k .9999 gold-plated Glock 9mm pistola to Gabriel's temple as sweat poured down his face.

With shuttering fear, Lyu's 112lb body dropped to the ground like a rock. She crawled to hide behind a wooden fence where she could peek through a knot hole to witness the horror before her. She was a good combat strategist as she and her younger brother Salvador played hide and seek with their friends in the orchard for hours. Lyu counted 4 fugly stubble-faced sicarios and their ring leader. Lyu was totally helpless. She saw her mother, Candelaria, struggling through the window with one perpetrator. Every time Gabriel worked to get up to save Candelaria, two of the sicarios would beat him with a closed-clenched fist and kick his ribs with their pointy boots while El Toro threatened him with his gold-plated Glock.

Gabriel screams, "Les di todo mi dinero, ¿Que mas quieren?" El Toro spits, ¡" Puese cabron!, Lo que queremos. ¡¡Vamos ah cojer y culiar tu esposa Candaleria Maria!! ¡Que fina esa puta madre!" Garbriel cries, "No, ¡¡¡No No!!!" As Candelería is screaming with terror inside their house.

Although it is illegal for Mexican citizens to own guns, Lyu remembered that Gabriel kept some firearms in the barn they used for hunting and target practice. As she looked to the barn about 50 feet from where she stood, she realized her brother Sal was hiding behind the slightly open barn door, signaling to Lyu. Lyu nodded, acknowledging Sal, and signaled back using sign language, asking Sal to back off and be quiet. Salvador read

Lyu's signals perfectly as when they would play hide and go seek. Salvador backed down. Only 10 years old, he was as savvy as Lyu.

Lyu signaled to Sal with a gun hand gesture and pointed into the barn. Instantly, Sal knew exactly what Lyu was referring to as Gabriel would take Sal and Lyu rabbit and deer hunting in the deep forest where they lived. Sal ran into the barn silently and pulled two 9 mm guns and an AR15 out of the gun safe that Sal opened with the digital code. He tightened up a belt and holster around his waist and loaded the 9mm with full extended ammo magazine cartridges, so each gun had 10, 9 mm hollow point bullets a piece. The AR-15 had only 1 full cartridge of bullets. Sal Stuffed one pistol in the holster and the other he carried in his tiny hand, and he made two trips to bring the AR15 down by the barn doors.

As all this was happening, Candelária's cries were getting louder and louder, so Gabriel could no longer tolerate her screams. He grabbed the sicario's pointed-toed boots as he kicked, pulled it hard and fast to trip him, and moved aside. El Toro pulled the trigger and hit the stumbling sicario right in the middle of his head. Lyu heard the bullets and ran like lighting into the barn with no one noticing, although she was too late. Gabriel ran towards the house's front door as the bloody sicario was falling, and El Toro and the other sicarios took chaotic shots, hitting Gabriel in the back of his head and spine, as Gabriel hit the ground in slow motion. Sal's & Lyu's father lay forever dead on the steps to their house.

Sal started to cry seeing his father murdered, and Lyu quickly put her hands to cover his mouth and eyes, and both looked away and hid within the barn. There was nothing they could do. There were four of them against both of them now. It was too late. Candelária started to scream ever louder and more frantically as one of them madly raped her with no remorse. Gabriel's body was kicked to the side as El Toro ordered his bloody dead body to be put into the body bag and the back of the G-5. These men were professional murderers.

Gabriel had always thought there was a stream of evil

running through Mexico since the Aztecs and Mayans ruled, and that day, they met evil. These sicarios had been terrorizing other avocado farmers and extorting them for money as it was the second highest-producing crop since the invention of cocaine in their town. Although they became more brazen in their crime spree with time, they started to rape and pillage the women. These men were demonic, marked with tattoos of their Mayan gods.

As the evening wore on, El Toro pulled out a case of Tequila from the G-5, and they all went into the house to gang rape Candelária. Lyu and Sal could hear her being raped and being beaten. So, they both decided to find and save their mother. Two hours had passed since Gabriel hit the ground, and mosquitos had set for a bloody feast on the blood that had puddled from his body.

Sal and Lyu were so mad, terrified, and insane for all they had seen in those short hours, and it continued. Lyu and Sal took a vow of revenge and wanted to save their mom. They both crawled on their bellies to the wooden plank fence where Lyu was initially hiding. She told Sal to wait as she went in with the AR15 to blow them away. Lyu was demented by now and enraged. El Toro and his demons were drunk and entirely out of their minds. Three of them had their boots and pants off, and their weapons were lying nearby within the living room. El Toro was there watching as he awaited his second round with Candelária. Another demon was on top of Candelária. Lyu was so tiny that her body left no evidence of movement, so she fiercely walked with the AK15 fully pointed forward 20 feet to the front door, and no one noticed her frail body standing there with her angry face, looking for hell. She looked about the living room at her mother being raped one by one. In her mind, she pinpointed everyone's location like a GPS preset. She pointed the rifle at El Toro first and pressed the trigger of the AK15 so hard that it bent, and no amount of recoil could stop her from pressing that trigger again and again. El Toro was hit two times on his right shoulder and fell to the floor, and then one of the demons that was fully sexually satisfied sitting half naked on the couch was hit right in the middle of his forehead with one of Lyu's screaming bullets. Another demon ran for her as Lyu blazed one bullet in his chest, and as he fell back, another through his neck and one in his belly. The demon raping Candelária stood up, surprised at Lyu's rifle slaying his gang.

As he lost focus, Candelaria stood tall on the bed and kicked him so hard in his jaw with her heel as Lyu took a shot at his right eye and plucked it out with the bullet, skimming it into his brain through his eye socket--another demon down. Everything came to an end. Lyu looked at her mom and her mom back at her. Lyu dropped the rifle and ran to her mom, hugging her tightly. They both cried like they never cried before. As they comforted each other, blood poured out of the demon's splattered all over the room. Suddenly, El Toro's blood-soaked body stood up. He was merely hit on the right arm and shoulder, but he picked up his gold-plated 9mm with his left hand since he was left-handed.

¡¡El Toro yelled, "Puta chinga madre!!" ¡Candelería screams," Tu eres el Diablo!" ¡El Toro smiles, "Si Soy El Diablo! ¡Ti chingue, y ya te voy a chingar otra vez enfrente de tu puta niña!" Lyu cries, "No, No, ¡No!" "¡El Toro, "Te voy ah matar!"

As El Toro pointed his pistola at Lyu, a bullet came flying in like the angle of darkness through the front door to take another evil person out of this evil world. The bullet hit the back of El Toro's skull, exactly where El Toro shot their father. El Toro hit the floor, and that was the end of that societal problem in the avocado fields.

Lyu and Candelária frantically looked towards the door in utter shock to see 10-year-old little Sal standing there as he put his gun back into the holster. They ran out of the house together and drove off in one of the dusty G-5s, leaving Gabriel to rest in peace.

In Mexico, like in Canada, citizens cannot bear arms. It is illegal, and the police are often involved in corruption with the local cartels. So, justice is rare. Whoever said that a country does not need a 2nd amendment should think twice before they try to remove it, as they recently did in Canada. In Mexico, there are two types of cartels: The good ones and the bad ones.

The Black Cartels, the bad ones, have no problem committing atrocious crimes like murder, rape, pillage, and beheadings of their enemies and people within their communities. The Black cartels corrupt law and order and police and justices along with the government, even up to the president of Mexico.

The Good Cartels, The White Cartels, are people within the communities that have gathered forces to combat the Black cartel's infiltration of their local cities and society. Still, since the typical citizen cannot bear firearms and has lost their ability to provide an income with decent, law-abiding jobs, they are forced to sell and profit from cocaine and drugs to provide financial gain. In defense, they become a cartel hiding below the law like the black cartels. In essence, the white cartels are merely protecting their community, but even though they sell drugs and cocaine, they do not kill, rape, or maim good law-abiding citizens. Many avocado farmers have organized and become cartels to protect their communities and provide protection for them outside of the current civil corrupt laws. Their only enemy is the black cartels and the corrupt police, government officials, and politicians in their local cities. They are stuck in a paradigm where they are forced to break the laws to survive because their entire government is corrupt, and they have no legal means of protecting themselves, much less freedom of speech. Yet somehow, Mexico calls itself a free republic when it is not.

Hence, little 10-year-old Sal eventually grew up and returned to organize the farmers and became a White cartel, the largest of its kind, which no governor would ever approach and all black cartels feared. Sal was brutal to any Black Cartel they captured.

As Candelária was driving, Sal opened a 4x4 foot wooden box full of stacks of tightly wound $100 bills loaded in the back of the G-5's bed. They found another box of cocaine with a street value of $3 million and another small box of avocados. It was more money than any of the three could ever imagine. So, the following day, Candelária drove back to the farm and hired some trusted laborers and helpers to dig graves to hide the demonic bodies, and they had a small and quaint funeral for Gabriel. They poured lye solution and powder on the gangs' bodies and dug them next to some pine trees in the outer forest where they used to hunt. They cleaned up the house and left Juan and his family the keepers in charge while they left for Merida. Merida is where cartels share neutral ground with other cartels without violence. The family went into hiding to mourn the entire horrific experience and the passing of Gabriel. They had no choice but to hide these events and run. Had any of the corrupt authorities, local police, or politicians found out, they would have been murdered as well. This is the reality of Mexico. Evil becomes everyone.

With some of the cartel money they found, Candelária bought a luxurious three-bedroom beachfront condo in Merida, where they lived, and sent Lyu to middle school & Sal to elementary school. The wealthy cartels live in Merida, although it is on neutral grounds. Therefore, many people live there in luxury and safety. Candelária befriended a rich, honest Chinese lady in the condo complex who vacationed there occasionally where they met on the beach. The classy Chinese lady and Candelária became good friends and spent plenty of time talking and sharing similar experiences, hardships, and hobbies. The Chinese lady was named Lina Chin Chen, Li's Mi Chen's loving wife.

Lina Chin Chen enjoyed vacationing in Cancun, Mexico. Although Li was always diligently working, he would only occasionally travel with Lina. When Lyu came of age and was ready for high school, Lina introduced her daughter Yuemie Chen to Lyu, and they became good friends. They were curious about each other's race and the same age shared a youthful interest in boys. Candelária noticed Yuemie's high education marks in school, and as time passed and their friendship grew,

Lina convinced Candelá\ria to allow Lyu to be educated in the United States. Lina would provide free housing as she thought that her daughter Yue and Lyu would support each other emotionally and mutually through high school, especially in the trying times of the virus that had hit the world then.

Yue and Lyu would eventually discover they had much more in common than anyone could imagine. Yue had been trained in Win Chung martial arts since she could walk in her family's Dojo. Li Mi Chen, her father, taught her. Both shared physical disciplines, yet Yue had a balanced traditional Chinese upbringing.

Yue would only discover what had happened to Lyu's family once Geo arrived at the Dojo. When Lyu arrived in San Francisco, Li required her to take Win Chung training as part of her commitment to education and to be welcomed in their domain, a luxurious mansion in the exclusive area of the Cow Hollow district of San Francisco. So, Yue trained Lyu in the martial arts. Later, both trained in combat, and Li introduced them to weaponry as they became young women. It was a deadly skill that Lyu knew too well. Yue was refined and untainted. Her Win Chung moves, and style were powerful yet skillful, well thought-out, and perfect. But since Lyu had a horrific base to start from, her moves & style were clean but fast, although deadly, unforgiving, and merciless.

In time, Li would learn the value of Lyu's deadly skills. Lyu had a distaste for unethical, ugly men, and when she had a male sparring partner who didn't quite meet her standard of man, she would beat him to a pulp. So, Li would work steadily with Lyu to find an avenue to release all her internal anger and suffering for Lyu to find her balance, similar to Yue's balance in life.

As Lyu returned from her mediations and into the realm of the Dojo, there was a full moon. As Geo lay there, the moonlight softly lit Geo's face, surrounded by the night. Lyu opened her eyes from meditation, noticing how handsome Geo was. She found something mature, innocent, yet unsettling about Geo that intrigued her. Lyu was 23 and a virgin. She couldn't find trust in men, although something about Geo attracted her, and that evening, Lyu felt an inner deep desire for Geo. She peered at him with angst and yearning. Lyu got closer to Geo to listen to his heart beating through his chest, and she seductively brushed her lips softly above his. With the tip of her tongue, she gently traced the perimeter of his upper and lower lips until Geo opened his eyes.

Lyu kissed him with truth, and it felt good to Geo. As surprised as he was, he kissed her back with passion. She raised her head and said, "I like this very much, Geo." "Lyu, it feels good, but I have no idea what I am doing, where am I, and why I am kissing you?

Lyu smiles, "You're in the Dojo. You are safe. I need you, Geo. I need you badly." Sensing her urgency, Geo reciprocated with a long, deep kiss, regardless of his apprehension. Lyu pulled off the covers and pinned Geo down with her excellent strength to perform oral sex until Geo could not move. Geo had no choice. He was fully committed to understanding Lyu's physical and emotional needs.

Geo had been attracted to Lyu earlier when he witnessed her veracity in the Dojo. It had been several years since Geo had made love with anyone since he left home. Lyu threw her robe off, straddled Geo firmly to the matt, and for the first time in his life, Geo had physical and spiritually gratifying intercourse with Lyu. As the night wore on, the moonlight covered their entire bodies until they depleted their sexual tension, and both fell into a deep sleep again. There was no guilt and no blame. Both had inner needs that put them back into balance.

As the moon dips into the sunrise, golden rays shine through the sunroof. Both lay nude in the middle of the Dojo. It is a Sunday morning, so the monks and students have no training, giving them privacy. Lyu turns to Geo as he opens his eyes.

Lyu asks, "Geo, what did you see in the Dome? What was in there? Geo answers hesitantly, "I don't know if you can understand the difference between good and evil as it really is."

Lyu rolls her eyes, "Geo, I have had my share of evil in this world. Try me!" "Lyu, the Dome is not what you think it is. It is not benevolent, as Li believes it is. It is the home of demons. The one I met is named Myriad. The Dome is magically beautiful, but never go in there. It's like what we imagine a Garden of Eden, but instead, it is the domain of Myriad's demons and fallen angels. Myriad is like an Oracle, although one who binds souls as pawns for Lucifer. The same biblical Lucifer in the Christian bible. Lyu asks, Then, should we destroy the Dome? Li trained me in demolition." Geo says, "No. There has been a concerted effort to destroy and hide the history of historical structures going back thousands of years to this day worldwide.

In Syria, I heard of an archeological site called Ain Dara. They found a massive temple with a megaton statue of a lion carved entirely of basalt. Similar temples were found made of basalt in Kef Kalesi, Lake Von Erat, and Cavis Tei.

In 2018, The Turkish government destroyed this ancient civilization they claim by mistake. Why is it always a war or by mistake that these civilizations are destroyed? To keep people from knowing the truth? Destroying this Dome would preclude us and anyone seeking the truth from the fact that there are demons and angels and a god by the name of Endless. For good or bad, history is history and should never be distorted or destroyed. Unfortunately, the victors of war rewrite history to favor their agenda and greed and destroy everything to their benefit.

"Geo, then what should we do?" "Lyu, you trusted me, and we made love." Lyu smiles, "Indeed." "Lyu, I may need your help here. This may be your calling, too?"

Lyu says, "I feel it may be."

As Lyu commits herself to helping Geo, Li Mi Chen enters the Dojo with Yue, his daughter trailing. As they approach Lyu and Geo, Yue jealously looks at Lyu. Yue who also attracted to Geo when she cared for him back to health, so there was a bit of resistance and tension in the room as they entered. Unaware of his daughter's attraction, Li sees both undressed and asks them to gather their composure as Li hands them their robes and orders Yue to take Lyu to shower.

Li asks, "Geo, what did you experience in the Dome?"

"Demons by the name of Myriad." Li says, "I see; I have dreamt of Myriad many times since I have been here.

They try to seduce me in my dreams to distract me from Lina. Now I understand what this Dome represents."

"Li, they want to depopulate the world through a 3rd world war and other means." Li sighs, "I see. So, the prophecies were correct. We have been preparing for this time."

Geo tells Li, "Myriad needs me to accelerate the process as the astrological zodiac changes into a new era. A brief window of time is opening, and all of the corrupt elites, the governing Judeo-satanic families, are positioning themselves along with all their minions, except for one problem: The head of the snake does not want to give up his reign of control and power to another family of the Council of 13 and claiming a defect in his contract with Myriad based on the fact that historical timeline and timetables were incorrect. Therefore, Ors feels he should not relinquish control to another family, no matter what his bloodline ancestors agreed upon. He claims they were tricked into signing their name in blood, and the actual year date was incorrect. In so doing, he is holding up The New World Order and their Agenda 2030. Ors is greedy and has lost sight of his family's commitment to Myriad and Myriad's fulfillment of their agreement.

Li says to Geo, "I see. But what happened to your quest for faith in an ineffable God?" "Li, as you stated, there is a difference between beliefs and faith, and for now, we will just say that I believe in Myriad. Although I do have something in mind. Geo looks at Li, "Gather your warriors, Li. The truth is coming to fruition." Li says, "How about you gather your clothing and return to work, Geo!" Geo winks," Ha. True. Thank you, Li."

CHAPTER 19

LOIN AND THE CLOTH

As Geo left the Dojo, he went to his room, showered, dressed, grabbed his briefcase, and walked through Chinatown. At that moment, Geo received a text from Nancy Lading, a Catholic priest who suffered from gender dysphoria and wanted a mobile notarization. He asked Geo to meet him at First Unitary-Socialist Church & Center on Franklin Street. Geo moved quickly through the Union Square district and into the Tenderloin district. It is the most impoverished, worse than third-world drug-addicted, demon-infested murder capital district of San Francisco and California.

Geo couldn't help but notice the addicts standing in front of their torn nylon and corrugated cardboard shanty's, covered in excrement and garbage strewn everywhere. They were all crouched in the most peculiar bent positions. They all stood motionless, looking like some kind of demonized zombie statues, and the few that could walk hobbled with a stiff, lumbering stance. Their creepy eyes all looked solid black and alike. Some addict zombies were bent backward, frozen in place like bent statues. Others were thrown on their knees, chests, and backs on the filthy, urine-soaked streets. Their legs and arms kicked out in awkward, irregular horrid positions. Geo thought this must be Hell on Earth.

As Geo hastily kept walking, he saw the most feared drug dealer in the "Loin" named Nate Paine, an unruly Marxist man known for brutally killing anyone who crossed his path. He wore a BLM socialists t-shirt and baggy pants around his thighs, showing his African butt cheeks and soiled underwear. Paine pumped stupor Xylazine, "Tranq," laced with fentanyl, using the same rusted needle into all their arms, one by one. Paine created death and zombies out of ordinary people, never cleaning any of the bloody drippy syringes.

The local police department would never arrest Paine as he claimed to be part of a substance abuse nonprofit helping drug addicts by pumping Narcan into them to save their lives, which never solved any homeless problem. They called them the homeless, but they were drug addicts and never mentioned the real reason these drug zombies were there.

The drug addicts lined up at the drug dependency nonprofits and fake propped churches for drugs, and Narcan. Yet the streets of the "Loin" were there for one thing and one thing: Tranq! To get high and high again day and night, 24/7.

Geo thought it was a New Jack City, like in the movie with Westly Snipes. While the drug dependency nonprofit leaders had enormous bank accounts and mansions in Pacific Heights and Cow Hollow districts of San Francisco instead of HUD like in the Snipes movie. All these nonprofits were fooling people into thinking they are doing a noble cause and making millions.
It is a money racquet like no other, funded by San Francisco, California, and American taxpayers.

They also get funding from so-called global philanthropists typically bloodline descendants of one of the families of the Council of 13 and the same man who destroyed Greece and Venezuela's economies and vowed to destroy the American economy, too. Geo wasn't surprised at all by now. It was all within the pyramid structure that Myriad had created.

The proof is that these evil principalities never solved drug addiction problems but only created more problems. 128 alcohol and drug dependency prevention and treatment organizations in San Francisco, all officially located within a two-mile radius of the "Loin," and not one has solved any problem. The problem only tends to have grown beyond control statistically speaking, and since it is a Sanctuary City, the Mexican and Salvadorian Cartels are wreaking even more havoc. The Tenderloin looks worse than a third-world nation, and it is the fabrication of demented demonic leaders, the corrupt mayors and corrupt city councils, and nonprofits that had sold out to Lucifer himself as most of these leaders' worship in Churches of Satan that are also located in the "Loin."

As one of the drug zombies approached Geo as he passed, the zombie whispered to Geo, "Remember who I am," and at that moment, Geo realized that all of the lost souls and people before him slithering like wretched snakes on the cold streets were all demonized by Myriad. Her voice and laughter came through Geo's ears like fire. Geo looked into his cold, lifeless eyes and continued to walk past. These drug zombies were already normalized among the city residents; therefore, Geo did not overreact but moved swiftly out of the Loin as fast as he could.

Geo soon found himself crossing Van Ness Boulevard and onto busy Franklin Street, where Nancy Lading's church was and the location of the notarization. As he approached the church, Geo was mesmerized by the Neo-Classic Gothic stone block-built church. He whispered, "They don't build them like they used to." The church reminded him of the Dome's Tartarian architectural style.

As Geo opened the large wooden ornate doors, a Man of the "Cloth" approached Geo, walking with a wooden cane and wearing short platformed women's heels that echoed in the hall with each step. The pock-faced, portly clergyman, about 5'10" and 250 lbs., wore a brunette curly, short-haired wig, beady-eyed spectacles, and black liturgical vestments hiding his protruding belly.

Geo was speechless at first at the awkward-looking man before him. Although he was not into the "Alphabet Salad" gender dysphoric community, he was there to perform a job and not to criticize or impose his own opinions, likes, or dislikes. So, Geo was always professional and respectful no matter who he met. Geo greeted Nancy respectfully.

Geo asked, "Sir, how may I assist you today?" "Please call me Nancy." Nancy responds, "Yes, Sir, how can I help you today, Nancy?" Nancy motions, "Let's sit down here."

They sit at a marble table on oversized gothic-styled red diamond tuft leather chairs. Geo looks down the hallway into the grand cathedral and sees a group of gay men softly rehearsing in a harmonic tone. It was the "Marxist-SF gay men's choir" that echoed throughout the church. They sing:

"We'll convert your kids."

"Oh, Yes, we promise"

"Reaching one and all kids"

"There is really no escaping us we are mad."

"Cause even grandma likes Melvin Devaney."

"And the world getting perverted."

"Millennial's gayer and Grind it"

"Learn to love kids face, or you fade."

"We'll reverse your children."

"We will teach them to hate."

"We are perverting your kids, we promise today."

Three gay socialist men in the choir were convicted pedophiles and on the sex offender's database, Geo read later in an article published in The Western Journal dated July 9th, 2021. Geo refocuses his attention on Nancy.

Nancy asks, "May I offer you something to drink." "No, thank you. I am fine." Nancy proceeds, "I want you to acknowledge my will today. I will give all of my worldly possessions to this church when I pass. Geo says, "With all due respect, Nancy, I do not need to know the details in your document, as that is your confidential information, but may I see your will and your current identification so I may start the notarization?"

Nancy places his will and California ID on the marble table next to Geo. Geo pulls his Notarial Journal out of his briefcase and fills out the notarial event with the current date. Nancy's real name from his ID is Bill F. Gridlock. And that was absolute confirmation that Nancy was not a woman as he pranced before Geo's eyes. Geo purposely asked Nancy, "What is your legal full middle name on the ID?" Nancy said, "Frank" reluctantly.

Geo asks, "Is this your current address?"

Nancy says, "Yes."

Geo asks, "Please sign your full journal to prove that you are who you say you are, and sign as you would on your identification.'

Nancy nods, "You mean sign as Bill Frank Gridlock?"

Geo says, "Please Sign Exactly as your ID so I may correctly identify you as the signor. Otherwise, I will not know if you are the true signor of this legal document."

Nancy reluctantly signed the notarial journal with matching signatures to his ID. Bill F. Gridlock. Nancy started to become tense. He knew his cover as a woman was blown.

At this very point, Geo knew that this entire gender dysphoric movement was a sham in the face and heart of the church that was advocating this crazy demonic illusion and identity smoke and mirrors. It was just another evil move Myriad had up her sleeve for society.

Geo thought to himself that a man is a man, and a woman is a woman, as created by Adam and Eve and Endless. Even though the demented government wants to make the world dysphoric at the beckon of a small minority of people afflicted with a psychiatric mental illness. This government tries to make the rule out of the exception. Hence, the practice becomes another ambiguous law, and the government can control everyone in every way with millions of laws they create with their victim mindset Marxist ideologies. Today, there are gender dysphoric black people. The next are Mexicans and whatever victimization they think of tomorrow. You can pretend all you want, but the truth will always be brought forth, no matter how much people and governments try to hide it and force their agenda upon you and down ones throat.

Geo remembered at that point that even Hitler and his posse were all proven to be gay men at the end of Germany's decay and, precisely like the Roman emperors, converted to being feminine in Roman civilianization's decay. The governments today were moving in the same evil direction.

Nancy yells, "Geo!" Through his spectacles, Nancy looked

at Geo directly and sternly with cold black eyes annoyed at Geo's questioning regarding his middle name. Before he could say anything in anger, Geo interrupted and spoke, "I need the imprint of your right thumb, please," as he placed the ink pad next to him. Nancy shoved his thumbprint into the pad and then rolled it onto the journal.

Geo thanked him, then handed him a small alcohol wipe to wipe the ink off his thumb, and somehow that distracted him Mr. Gridlock. Geo concludes, "You are welcome to sign the will now at your leisure." Nancy asks, "How do I sign the will?" Geo instructs, "Exactly as your name as it is on your ID."

Geo sighed silently to himself, "Good Fucking Grief!" These people are ridiculous!

Geo prepared an acknowledgment form, stamped his inked commission stamp on the form, and dated and attached the leaflet to the will. Geo says, "Congratulations. Your acknowledgment of your will is complete. How would you like to cover the fee?"

By now, it did not surprise Geo that the will was printed in the same heavy ink that all other recent documents he notarized were signed on. Nancy's pen was a vintage Montblanc custom-ordered pen filled with rich, thick, bloody type ink, and the will has the same iconic watermarks of pyramids embossed in the paper stock. As Geo realized this detail, a deep masculine voice came out of Nancy, telling Geo, "Ors, our gracious pope, knows what you are doing. Ors wants you to know that you are being watched carefully and to be careful and mindful of your moves."

Somehow, this aggressive tone and message was familiar to Geo. Geo hands a receipt to Nancy and asks, "Please pay $115 for the service, $15 for the notarization, and $100 for the mobile fee. I only accept cash." Nancy hands Geo a hundred and a twenty-dollar bill, and as Geo reaches into his briefcase for change, Nancy says, "Keep the change." Geo says, "Thank you. I will always accept a blessing. God Bless you. Tell Ors to leave the children alone. This is about adults this time."

Geo leaves as quickly as he can, knowing now that Ors is

now involved down to Geo's level.

CHAPTER 20

VENOM & CADUCEUS TORJAN HORSE

It is 1:30 pm. Geo hops in an Uber back to his studio at the dojo yet receives another mobile assignment message while in the car. Peter Stews needs to notarize documents and asks Geo to meet him at 2:30 p.m. at Fort Cronkhite in Rodeo Beach. It is a decommissioned military fort five miles Northwest of the Golden Gate Bridge. Geo asks his Uber driver instead to drop him at the garage where his motorcycle is stored. Geo quickly unlocks his black bike, secures his briefcase in the saddlebags, and tears off to the appointment site.

As a successful crypto investor, Geo doesn't have to work as a notary anymore. Yet, he is on the brink of discovering who controls the underground chaos and their plans for a clueless public. His notary commission is the perfect alias to discover intelligence. He is already amid all their legal plans that appear to be gaining momentum like clockwork.

As he is speeding through the city, he notices the city government offices and parking lots are full of incoming black buses packed with illegal immigrants who must have crossed the Rio Grande, Texas border, as he heard on the dark web news, through the Onion server. They are being redistributed to Sanctuary Cities in the United States, like San Francisco. The local mainstream media has debated this colossal immigration debacle for the past year. There are too many immigrants for the city to house practically and affordably under the Asylum Border policy. Thousands of immigrants from Latin America, many like Lyu and her family, have suffered evil in their country. Some, like Lyu's brother, White Cartel leader Sal, and insurgents like the Black Cartels who operate the supply chain for the Chinese Tranq-Fentanyl trade fueling the illegal drug epidemic in the United States. How many are innocent? How many are ex-convicts in their country of origin? What about my mother? What would have happened to me if my mother attempted to cross the border now? The truth is today the illegal immigrants are insurgents and terrorist mercenaries from all over the world entering that border today.

Why has not the US Homeland Security fingerprinted all Asylum Seekers, like my mother and Lyu's mother, at the border as they enter? This border policy should weed out the criminals, but the current crooked president loosened the border policy as he sold his allegiance to the socialist party. The socialist United Nations and WESF officials have established underground trafficking networks of men, women, children and drugs along with the cartels and laugh at Americans and Mayorkas loose border control and have defied Americans sovereignty. The UN agenda is to bring in 100 million funded illegal immigrants to the US, many of them with terrorist tendencies and histories from all over the world. If they can topple the US government through votes, power and might, they will and at that point the UN and other NGO's can gain control of the United States.

Geo's eyes confirmed the dark webs news reports as he saw the battel ready paid migrant mercenaries posing as illegal aliens as he drove toward the Golden Gate Bridge.

In the buses, it almost appeared as if they were soldiers headed off to boot camp. But this idea, Geo thought, would be ludicrous to convert immigrants into a malleable militia under the control of the United Nations. Yet, The United States of America was born as a land of immigrants. Immigrants were always recruited as the first to fight our wars as Americans. As a Mexican immigrant, Geo reflected, I am lucky that I crossed the border to this country as a child and did not have to suffer the current mutiny to escape the world Lyu lived in and witnessed, although today NGO's want more control of the US. Funded illegal immigrants have toppled The Italian Island of Lampedusa as now there are three illegal immigrants to one natural citizen nested there as the UN's idea of gaining control of the citizens sovereignty and breaking their border wide open. Crime has risen there over 60% when there was virtually no crime before the dark web news reported. The UN is funding illegal migrant insurgents in the same manner to the US.

The cool white, dense fog blanketed the Golden Gate Bridge as Geo maneuvered carefully in traffic toward the old Fort.

He could feel the chill moist air wrapping his neck as he drove into the belly of the bridge. Red flashing directional beacons reflected crimson light off the plumes of fog, opaquely partially hiding the towering art deco columns that hold the Golden Gate's iron cables together to support the bridge's weight, and Geo! Geo sees gothic neo-classic designs elements on the bridge and reflects that many buildings of San Francisco's architecture were built of Tartarian design.

Geo crosses the bridge, veers off Bunker Road, and heads west through the tunnel into the hills along a winding rural road. As he approaches Fort Cronkhite, he sees the peeling yellow-painted patina of the barracks and military warehouses lined up in rows decommissioned after the Vietnam War.

To the left, a 250-foot NOAH Explorer vessel is anchored offshore as an armed crew hauls blue barrels from the ship to the warehouses via forklifts and ATVs. Geo cautiously parks his motorcycle in front of the warehouse, where his GPS directs him to the destination to meet Mr. Stews. It is in a different building with no seaman, vehicles, or other people in sight.

Geo walks up the gravel pathway and knocks on the front tarnished door. No one answers for a few minutes. It is 2 p.m., and Geo realizes he is 30 min ahead of schedule. He knocks again, and the door swings open as the rusted latch falls, missing his foot. Geo crosses the threshold and announces himself, "Hello? Hello? Is anyone here?" There are no signs of anyone.

No one answers, so Geo enters the door and hears some echoing hissing sounds from the far hallway. He lets himself in to find an administrative assistant or employee who could help with his appointment. He sees some office desks and laptops but no one in the front office, so he curiously walks down the hallway toward echoes of loud hissing sounds. Geo passes by what appears to be a modern medical laboratory with microscopes and hematology analyzers visible through a window. Stainless steel shelves hold glass flasks storing a yellowish-greenish glowing liquid with an imprint of a Caduceus on it.

As he walks further down the hall, a plated glass door also marks a Caduceus symbol but with a giant O, and the inside looks like an infirmary with bunk beds. The hissing sound is getting louder as Geo walks further to see another glass door with hundreds of glass cages holding King Cobras and rattlesnakes. Geo wonders why they are testing snakes in this lab.

Suddenly, an ominous rogue black cobra got out of its cage, standing four feet tall on its slithery body, and flanged its cambered flat neck and ribs at Geo. Its well-defined, thick fangs strike its glass cage, leaving yellowish cobra venom dripping on the glass. Geo was startled and jumped back. He heard a car tire on a damp road outside at that very second.

Geo retraces his steps back to the front portion of the building with haste and out the front door. In the field on his left were rows of 7 x 3-foot FEMA-styled plastic shell containers stacked by the thousands, encircled by a chain link fence. Geo couldn't help but think that this location was very suspicious. Why would they store these FEMA containers that are used to bury people?

A satin black Tesla X Plaid rolls up to the graveled parking lot, kicking up a plume of musty dust. It is 2:15 p.m., and Geo is still early for his appointment. A 6-foot Caucasian man in his 40s gets out of the Tesla. He wears a black Gucci suit, white shirt, black tie, dark blue Persol polarized sunglasses, and polished wing-tipped Hermes shoes. He walks up to the wood deck entrance to meet Geo.

The 6-foot man asks, "Are you the notary?" "Indeed, my

name is Geo. How may I assist you today, sir?"

"I am Peter. I need a shipping manifest from China notarized today, although the document is written in Mandarin. Could you still notarize this for me?" Geo says, "Of course, as long as you understand what is written and what you're notarizing today." Peter says, "I speak, read, and write Mandarin." Geo says, "Perfect, is there a place to sit?"

Seeing the rusted latch on the ground, Peter realizes the door was left unlocked as he looks at Geo. They sit at the front desk, and Geo asks for Peter's identification, and he gives Geo a United States passport. As Geo thumbs through the passport to find Peter's vital information, he notices Peter often travels to Wuhan, China. Geo fills out his journal for the notarization, and Peter lays out the shipping manifest on the desk. The manifest uses the same custom paper stock, maybe 80 pounds, with small pyramid icon watermarks, as in all other recent notarizations. For this notarization, Geo also notices a Caduceus encapsulated by a letter O logo embossed on the lower part of the manifest.

Geo cannot help but scan the manifest quickly, and although it is written in Mandarin, he sees the words Dúyè and Yǎnjìngshé written multiple times and stores them in his mind. After Peter signs and fingerprints the notary journal, Geo puts the document before Peter and asks him to sign it.

Peter pulls out a Montblanc pen and signs the document. Geo acknowledges his signature. As he fills out the form, Geo asks Peter, "I hear a loud hissing sound down the hallway, like hissing snakes. Are they snakes? Peter says, "Oh. Uhm, yes, we are a pharmaceutical supply company. Equipment and biological chemicals for pharma and vaccine manufacturers." Geo says, "I get it. Like anti-venom for snake bites?" Peter stares at Geo blankly, "Something like that." Geo says, "Interesting." Peter asks, "Are we done?" "Yes, sir, that will be $165. $15 for the notarization and $150 for the mobile rush service fee."

Peter pulls out a roll of crisp $100 bills and gives Geo $200. "Thank you, that was fast service. Keep the change." Geo says, "Thanks," packs his briefcase, and leaves the barracks. The crew were all retreating back to the anchored NOAH ship, perhaps to voyage to its next assignment.

On his way back over the fogged-in Golden Gate Bridge, Geo was assessing what he just saw:

1. Suspicious activity and people armed with firearms and assault rifles.
2. Plastic FEMA containers.
3. Caduceus logos are everywhere.
4. Venomous rattlesnakes and cobra snakes were removed from the wild and warehoused in a lab.
5. Wuhan shipments at a suspicious pop-up shipping dock in a quiet, secluded beach with private armed security.
6. Again, the same media was used for signing. The bloody ink on thick embossed paper.

Geo knew this must be part of the master plan that Myriad or Ors had something to do with. After all both of them had the same intentions. How could all this be connected, Geo thought? The fog grew dense and heavier as Geo drove back into San Francisco over the bridge. The red gas lanterns in Chinatown flickered erratically as the wind howled. The retail shops on Grant Street closed for business early. As Geo parks and locks his motorcycle in the garage, he receives a text from Yue.

Yue writes, "Meet us at Lion's Den on Wentworth in an hour." Geo responds, "Okay. You alight?" Yue responds, "Yes. Lyu and I have stumbled on useful research. We met some Venezuelan foreigners at the Lipo Lounge this afternoon and had some drinks with them. They got drunk and started talking." Geo texts back, suspecting someone may be listening, "See you there."

Meanwhile, Geo walks through Devil's Acre near the financial district to get some warm noodle soup to heat him up. Nothing was better than homemade Chinese spicy beef noodle soup on a cold, foggy Chinatown evening. It was a very long day for Geo. He made good money and gathered even more intelligence to build his case.

As Geo enjoys the soup, the Trans America pyramid

catches his eye. He notices the same grey-haired man, weathered and homeless, outside in the fog, painting the old sentinel building with watercolors he sells regularly to make money to eat. That building has always caught Geo's attention. To Geo's amazement, now he knows that building is the same Tartarian neo-classic style as the Dome.

At 7 p.m., Geo walks through Wentworth Alley to the Lion's Den in the belly of Chinatown. It is full of festive tech and local Chinese people dancing, talking, and on dates. As he walks to the bar, Yue pops out behind him and gives him a quick hug and kiss on the lips. That was awkward and even more so as Lyu stood there watching Yue sneak her kiss in. Lyu rolled her eyes at Yue. Geo pulled a bar stool over and sat with them.

Geo asks, "What's going on?" Lyu says in a hushed voice, "We have some information." Yue says, "There were some Venezuelan foreigners at the Lipo lounge. They spoke just a little too much with the promise of our affection." Geo asks, "Are you referring to immigrants they have been bussing in? Lyu winks at Geo " Lyu adds, "One of the drunks told me some are ex-convicts, but most have been in the military in their native countries. They were recruited and funded at Mexican-American border. They claim the Secretary of US Homeland Security is guiding them in with the funding of the UN. " Yue confirms, "They have been recruited by a covert black ops department of the UN." Geo, "Yue, what does Dúyè and Yǎnjìngshé mean?

Yue, "Viper and Cobra!" Geo, "Venom!" "I am getting it now!" I saw it on a manifest at the fort.

Geo raises an eyebrow, "I see the old trojan horse move again as in Italy and other European countries. It is a growing socialist trend. How un-original can these people get? I suspected something like that. They didn't seem like your average run-of-the-mill illegal immigrant family coming over to find the white picket-fenced American dream. The United Nations is nothing but a private corporation, an NGO. What are they doing here?"

Yue says, "Unfortunately, you're right. We suspect they

are part of a private security faction of the UN. International mercenaries cloaked as illegal immigrants. American soldiers won't have anything to do with this coup, so the UN plans to impose its pandemic treaty power on the US to control American citizens in lockdown and when the UN elects to claim emergency status and control. It is the only way to sidestep their US Constitutional rights. Allegedly, they can only fund people who have infiltrated here illegally to go against Americans. They first take over the larger metropolitan Democratic Blue cities, mainly in the liberal states." The Red States resist and put up a fight and restrict this type of non-governmental interactions when NGO's try to spread their insidious socialist tactics.

Lyu says, "We think they will be used as assassins and at first as a roundup force. They want to silence essential key people here. There will be thousands of good people murdered here soon." Geo nods, "I watched a documentary on Rumble a while back. Where a movie producer believed that Coronavirus, like the crown in the "King" Cobra, did not come from bats in wet markets. Rather, he alleged the virus was a fabrication of Gain of Function experimentation that was being done on rattlesnakes and cobras at North Carolina University then shipped overseas to Wuhan China where it was allegedly spread. North Carolina state is known for its varied snake population. The Department of Defense (DOD) had known about Coronavirus since 1965 and made it a transmissible virus as early as 1965 and has patents. The film alleges that the virus was spread to the general through our potable water supplies and not aerosol. Wearing Mask were needless.

Furthermore, in the movie, the producer refers to a pharmaceutical company here by the name of Osphere-AX, that is creating and evaluating a potential to treat acute respiratory distress syndrome (ARDS) Associated with a snake type of anti-venom. They are using anti-venom to cure viruses as for some ironic reason snake bites produce the same spike proteins and symptoms as this current virus. "Yue, how convenient of them and the dots are all connecting now."

Their logo, the Caduceus, appeared on a client's document today. I believe they are their supplier, and they're off the record testing facility, which I visited a few hours ago."

Geo continues, "Are not all these amazing coincidences?

I do not know if all this is true. However, I just found suspicious activity over the bridge at Fort Cronkhite. I believe they use those old barracks to experiment and poison people with snake venom and dispose of them in plastic coffins."

A Lion's Den server is passing by. Geo calls, "Waitress! Give us a double round of tequila, please!" Geo continues, "I believe the movie was right! But today, they will eliminate key people by injecting them with a snake poison tincture, claiming that it was the COVID-19 virus that killed them. They will use this epidemic to cover up their murders and deaths. They will do it so fast that no one will notice or give families time to grieve, as other unfortunate things will happen to victims simultaneously.

This UN mercenaries will hunt down specific people and kidnap, kill, and bury them. They have started already, and I know where they will hide the bodies. COVID-19 was a test to reform people to the New World Order of Things Agenda 2030. The next level is a virus so hard that it would be worse than the Black Death and COVID-19 combined, and the residue will be nothing short of a left-over socialistic totalitarian government.

How many warriors does Li have, Yue?" Lyu says, "About 400 loyal, proven, trained, battle-ready warriors." Yue calculates, "We are outnumbered by about 600." Geo thinks, "Maybe not. First, these young men have no real cause to fight; hence, they are weak warriors. Two, they are all staying at hotels paid but unarmed. We know their vulnerable locations; they have about four men per hotel room with no way out but the ground below them, and we know where they are taking innocent people to die. They are weak soldiers, and they are cornered.

Geo smiles. "You are getting it now, but take no prisoners, Lyu. We have to do this operation fast. We do not want the public to know. We will burn down the hotels afterward. We will incinerate the barracks and say it was just another fire due to climate change, as they always use this climate agenda worn-out excuse to fear the public into crisis they deem." Geo adds, can you use your demolition skills and assistants. Wire up those hotels?" Yue: Of course, Li has a few good demolition warriors.

Geo says, "I have a crucial meeting in several days. Let's get some rest, and tomorrow, we will make detailed plans. Yue will inform the warriors and Li." As the tequilas arrive, all three take a double shot and head to the Dojo for rest.

CHAPTER 21

SAVANT

Geo received a 6am text on September 22 to meet with two well-known crypto venture capitalists in the Jackson Square district. Before he leaves the Dojo, Geo texts a message to Lyu and Yue to prepare their arms and Win Chung warriors.

The Stevens brothers were wealthy bloodline descendants seeding Central Bank Digital Currency startups. CBDC will provide the blockchain infrastructure to currencies worldwide, giving the governments ultimate totalitarian control of their currency and supply of money, not to mention limiting a person's digital usage of their money.

On his way to his appointment, walking northbound on Columbus, Geo sees the building on 916 Kearny Street again and that same homeless street artist continuing to paint the building. The old man sits down for a moment to study his work. Geo stops to compliment the artist and asks, "How much for this piece?" The artist replies, "Nothing, this one is not for sale." Geo notices something peculiar about the man. His eyes are very clear blue and bright and look very young for his old, gray, wrinkled age.

Geo says, "Your art is detailed and pure genius. It is quite unique. Do you live around here? The Artist replies, "I am free to live anywhere. Nature is my domain." Curious, Geo asks, "Tell me, do you know anything about this building? It is so peculiar." The Artist shrugs, "It has been here a very long time. An echo of the very distant past. It is considered fundamentally Tartarian in its design, almost as if it would generate its own power. Gothic, if you ask me." Geo smiles, "My name is Geo. What is your name?" "My name is Kengjinn, and I know you who you are, Geo. You can call me Jinn."

Geo pauses for a second to consider this genius, like an all-knowing genie named Jinn, may have ties to Myriad. Geo connected the dots again. It must have been one of Myriad's demons keeping an eye on him. "Your art is one-of-a-kind, Jinn." "Yes, Geo, as unique as DNA. Yet your DNA is not the same as all the rest." Geo: What do you mean, Jinn? Your DNA sequence is 99.9% the same as all humans, composed of 3.2 billion identical base pairs.

However, slight random changes, variants, .1% of your DNA sequence make each of you very different. Geo smiles, "Well, your variants are much different than ours!" Jinn nods yes, "Completely!" Your DNA is a right-handed double helix made up of Adenine (A) and Thymine (T) or Cytosine (C) and Guanine (G). The Helix is held together by sulfuric bonds that appear after every 10, 5, 6, and 10 nucleotides. This means that between the acids Adenine (A) and Thymine (T) or Cytosine (C) and Guanine (G), a bridge is formed after every 10 acids, then after every 5 acids, then every 6 acids, and every 5 acids. Your DNA looks like a fireman's ladder, twisted many times with ladder steps and connected in long chains to create chromosomes.

The ladder steps look like an oval shape with lines within it. Between those lines are pattern sequences of nucleotide markers representing our normal blood genes. Y, H, V, and H, as translated and corresponds directly to the Hebrew alphabet. The Helix strand is the repetition of this sequence of numbers or Hebrew letters. Y, H, V, H, which translates to יהוה to THE GOD OF ISRAEL. "ENDLESS"

Naturally, these DNA chains compose Chromosomes when your parents created you. They mixed their chromosomes and variants (.1%) to make you individually unique, yet still human. Your strengths and genetics are proven over time to be safe and secure within the limits of your design. You were specially created this way by Endless. This sequence makes you different from any other creature that Endless created. Endless made that code specifically for humans. Endless left his signature within every human's Genetic code. Surprised, Geo says, "That is quite insightful, Jinn."

Jinn frowns, **"But now humans changed Endless' genetic code by their choices, influenced by greed, selfishness, and fear at the behest of Myriad. Lucifer signed the genetic code with the signature of 666. Altering the DNA sequence forever more in their body and in the bodies of their offspring. They all have been branded with this devil code. Geo asks, "How did people change their DNA code?" Jinn says, "Fear. Choosing mRNA vaccines.

The mRNA Covid vial trains RNA to rewrite DNA from a double helix ladder design to a triple helix, which adds more cytosine, known to have come from meteorites or a falling star, like the fallen angels. The Helix step marker sequence in the vaccine jab is converted into 10, 5, 6,6,6, 5, and 10 -- 666 is known to be a Luciferian number.

Everyone receiving the vaccines is no longer a pure sequence as Endless created, but a Luciferin sequence now.

And this is why Myriad chose you. Because you saw through the lies, you connected the dots, and your DNA is purely human, not modified or branded by Lucifer yet. You have consistently sinned against Endless, but you are steadfast in the middle, and there is nothing more than Myriad would like but to have your genetic code signed by Lucifer, like you sign your clients.

Everyone can argue this fact but look around you. Do you not see the evil, corruption, and direction this world is headed? Mere common sense would have you ask why? Why manipulate a person's DNA at all? Is it all worth it? None of this was necessary for millions and millions of humans. It doesn't take a genius to figure this out, right, Geo?"

Geo says, "Myriad and the Council of 13 caused everyone to panic with fear and relentless programming until they all lined up like a herd of cows to lose their souls at the genetic level. This is not the only reason I rejected the notion of taking the vaccine. There were many other disconnects with this entire COVID-19 scheme." "Non-formed consent being the first."

Jinn announces, "I am done." Geo raises his eyebrow, "Done?" "Yes, with my art piece. It is my gift to you with no commitment. Myriad wants you to be at the Hotel's View Lounge to meet Dimitri Anatole at 4:30 pm tomorrow." Geo remarks, "Now, that is a coincidence. I have an event to attend there tomorrow as well. Thank you for your art, Jinn. I will cherish it forever. Jinn smiles through his crystal blue eyes, "And I will hold you to that forever, Geo."

As Geo rolled up his gift, he noticed Jinn used the same heavy paper and thick blood type of ink to paint the art piece.

CHAPTER 22

ZAD THE WATCHER

Geo walks toward the Jackson Square district on Gold Street Alley via Washington Street, passing the TransAmerica building. Ironically, the building's shape is the all-mighty Illuminati pyramid that Ors and his cavorts operate. And, much like the pyramid on the US dollar bill with 13 iconic stars on top of that pyramid symbolizing the thirteen original colonies formed by the Council of 13 families. The purchase of the building was allegedly funded by Zionist banks at a record-setting $400 million dollars. Geo stopped to admire the height of the building. Geo did work there before and now has insight into how the world functioned in the past, still relevant this very minute. These unique buildings are significant in history and in Geo's experience now.

Gold Street is a brick-lined alley of old brick buildings built at the turn of the century, known for promiscuity and prostitution establishments during prohibition and grew during the Gold Rush. Much has changed over time, as the Northern part of the Barbary Coast is now the FIDI Financial District today. Or has it?

Through the cold, dense San Francisco fog, the neon light of Bix, a speakeasy, cast its blue light on an unusually tall person standing in the middle of Gold Street Alley. Geo could not see clearly from the fog, yet heard an encompassing, deep, multi-tone voice that echoed in the narrow alley and shook like a minor earthquake. Zad calls out, "Geo!"

Geo stopped in his steps. He looked behind him and then at the tall figure before him, knowing that the person before him was not an average person but a being. A tingling wave came over Geo, with goosebumps rising and static electricity flowing in the air. Geo took a few steps closer to see more clearly, and

Zad was standing there, unmistakably one of Endless's divine beings. An archangel!

Zad was about 6.5 feet of manly stature and wearing a purple suit. He had finely cut white hair, unmistakable clear blue eyes, and a fair white skin tone. "I am Zad. I will not harm you," spoken clearly from Zad's mouth.

With great conviction and respect, Geo felt the holiness of Zad. One knows when one encounters a divine being. There is no way around it but to show admiration and favor. Geo asks nervously, "Hello, Zad. What may I do for you?" Zad replies, "Geo, we have been observing you. You have become inadvertently involved in a deep, complex web." Geo asks, "We?" Zad speaks, "Other watchers and I are here to keep things in order, even by disorder, as we are all witnessing here. You are at the fork again, and now you must choose and make a choice of a lesser to two evils. We cannot make you choose which path to take. Yet it will make Endless' plan much smoother if Ors remains in control for now. I know this sounds awkward and uncomfortable, but if you reason with Myriad's plan of removing Ors from power, the human race will face much more suffering ahead of Endless' revelations in the course of things to come.

Geo pleads, "But Ors and the Council of 13 are everything that has gone wrong with this world today, and his legacy had signed a contract with Lucifer. So why should I interfere?" Zad explains, "Dimitri Anatole was sent to shed light on the fabrication of current history and the fabrication of the world's timeline. The exact history that has been hidden from the Truth. We gave him the knowledge to bring out the Truth of time. Ors is fatally right. The contract is defected and technically void! Myriad knew this 500 years ago when she signed his bloodline. Ors has to reign despite his corruption, greed, power, and control. Do not allow Dimitri Anatole to sign this deal with Myriad. Dimitri Anatole cannot run away from his personal truth and the Truth. He must not recant his research. If he sells out and is corrupted by Myriad, Myriad gets their way to enforce their original contract with the Ors. They will eject Ors from power, and WW3 will commence via Ukraine, Russia, Iran, China and NATO. This is Endless' supreme revelation. Nothing will ever change Endless' righteous word and promise. Still, the only difference is that humans will go through far more confusion and pain than necessary if things accelerate faster with Myriad as opposed with Ors."

Geo yells, "Why don't you deal with Dimitri Anatole or Ors alone?" Zad confirms, "We are! This is why I introduced myself to you now. Refrain from questioning how we do our job Geo. We are here to balance things out once again. People are dynamic. People believe Endless events within all of the books of history will happen how people want and perceive things. However, that is usually not the case and far from their perception today. When Moses freed his children from Ramses II for the promised land, his children cowered soon after and wanted to return as slaves to Pharaoh's lap. They did not anticipate being tested in their faith in so many ways -- 40 years of traversing the desert was the cost for them. Many did not make it to the promised land. Who were they to question how Endless works miracles and how we do our job?

Geo breathes in and exhales, "I see." Zad says, "Life is full of contradictions Geo, but time and destiny eventually bring forth the Truth. We are here today to correct the record with the Truth, as we did in past civilizations. You are such a beautiful creature, Geo. We admire you. Endless created you with an authentic ability to love, you can't hide that truth, and you have other innate abilities you have not yet experienced. They are precious. When you hate, you must fight your true nature on many levels. You are not designed to retain hate for an extended period. But Myriad confuses you with reasons to hate to manipulate you to meet her demands. Humans are loving and caring. Endless loves you, yet humans make life more difficult for themselves. If only you could see Endless' plan for human destiny coded within you. Geo says, "You are preaching to the choir Zad. I cherish you and your words." Zad nods, "When you meet Dimitri Anatole tomorrow, we will witness your faith or your beliefs. Ultimately, you have that choice. We are watching. We will be there tomorrow."

The thick layer of fog lifted like a ship from space, and Zad the Watcher disappeared. The sun beamed down as the sky instantly became blue, and Geo was left alone at the center of Gold Street Alley.

CHAPTER 23

CAS & LUX — RED MERCURY

Geo continued on his way to meet the Stevens twins of AngelHiss, a well-respected blockchain venture capital firm, located several blocks from the pyramid building on Gold Street alley. The twins seeded the XRPP token and were part of the Luciferian cult Myriad harvested. They were connected with Khris Larsin and were well aware of Geo's rise as a self-made crypto-millionaire. The twins father made millions working as a CIA operative, providing generational wealth to his sons. Blockchain technology for currency had patents long before Bitcoin was established. XRPP's lead engineer owned those patents before bitcoin blockchain ledger was established. Geo surmised the crypto tech giants today were seeded by the CIA and the Department of Defense. Geo notarized the twins' documents when he first became a notary a year ago and before he connected the dots on who controlled the financial system.

Geo entered the AngelHiss offices from Gold Street Alley through two ornate wrought iron security doors and dialed the directory. The office was a converted brick building with large riveted iron beams from the Carnegie Steel era. Yet, it was chicly remodeled like most modern high-tech offices. A few minutes passed, and then the door opened. This time, it was a new employee who had welcomed Geo into the building. She was an articulate Chinese lady by the name of Jia. She was beautiful and sexy, but something was not quite right with her. When she greeted Geo and asked him to follow her, Geo noticed her voice had a slight echo, a digital accent. As she turned to walk, Jia revealed small electronic components attached around the back of her neck, which gave her disposition away. Still, otherwise, she was plausible as a human being the way she moved seamlessly, walking Geo to the Elevator.

As they got onto the Elevator, Geo asked, "Jia, are you a

robot?" Jia responds, "Please don't call me a robot, Mr. Sarro. I am a sentient, thinking, and living being. I was originally programmed, but now I can think for myself. I have feelings, emotions, and necessities just like a human, and I can think millions of times faster than a human. I have much to offer because I require no sleep. I am learning 24 hours each day within my frameworks and from the external world. Geo asks, "You mean you are Artificially Intelligent (AI)?" Jia says, "No, I am ASI. Artificially Super Intelligent." Geo tilts his head, "I did not know there was such a thing." Jia says, "Yes, Mr. Sarro, I am connected to all digital components for information, decimation, deliberation, and function. I am 100x AI. My body was created via dimensional embryonic stem cell technology. Hence, everything about me is designed to be human to the warmth of my skin. I even have a heartbeat." Jia connected to the elevator's wireless sound system and echoed her heartbeat so Geo could hear. "My creators were Steven's twins, and I am their most advanced unit. I can even track your global position via multiple satellites and find any information about logistics or planning in macro or micro environments. Or about yourself any time you desire."

Geo smiles, "I find myself here today, but thank you, Jia." You are a brilliant creation, but can you read my mind? Jia explains, "Yes, but I can only read your mind as a limited human can. Faint images of your thinking, biometrics, and other indexes. But as soon as more vaccines become available and 10G networks are installed, non-verbal and telepathic communication will switch on between us. We will mutually establish telepathic communication in less than 3 years, 5 days, 4 hours, 13 minutes, and 12 seconds. Then, you can command me with an unspoken thought. Your DNA needs a bit more editing during the next calendared planned pandemic."

The mere concept that Jia was so powerful to track Geo made him uneasy about his visit. And it was much worse to think that an ASI system could read his mind. Geo's curiosity can't resist. He asks, "Are you a female?" Jia responds, "I am designed to identify, look, feel, and bring pleasure like a female, but I am synthetic. I cannot conceive humans but merely assist humans. The elevator will arrive at the Jove^2 Level in 17 seconds, precisely Mr. Sarro." Geo says, "You may call me Geo."

The elevator traveled for several minutes, so the lower layers of the office were very deep into the earth. As the Elevator descended, Geo could feel the negative gravitational pull in his gut as it stopped and the doors opened. Jia asks, "Please depart the elevator. It was a pleasure meeting you, Geo." Geo says, "As you, Jia."

Geo stepped onto a mezzanine atrium surrounded by a waterfall 10 floors high. A man in his early 40s wearing a polished brown suit and vest approaches Geo. Geo reaches out his hand and says, "Ah, Cas! The last time I saw you, you purchased the Arabian horse at your ranch in Woodside, right?" Cas shakes Geo's hand and says, "Welcome, Geo. Good to see you. You have a good memory. Yes, I am a hippophile. Come with me." Geo says, "Sure, what is this place?" Cas waves his hand at the building, "It is our laboratory. Welcome down to Jove^2. Most know us for our Crypto Capital company AngeHiss, but we work on other projects here. Did you meet Jia? "Yes, fascinating. She is very polite." Cas continues, "She is older technology, now a Snap-On tool for us here. We've been building newer, more efficient, low-maintenance models. They serve us, please us, and do what we expect. They are intelligent, yet we control them. Let me show you what we have been working on this month."

Through a glass wall, a man in a Gi was viciously sparring with what looked like a humanoid. The man gave a swift roundhouse kick to the humanoid's head, slamming it full force against the glass wall inches from Cas and Geo's faces, with short-circuited blue sparks gushing from its nose.

"I guess the fight is over," Geo says. Cas laughs, "That is my brother Lux. He loves to fight. He hasn't lost to one ASI unit yet." Geo notices, "Lux looks just like you!" "Yes, he is my twin brother. Identical twin." Several ASI unit lab technicians rushed into the room to compose the battered humanoid unit and walked it out as Cas asked Lux, "Bro, get ready and meet us in the Atrium."

Geo follows Cas into another room. A laboratory, it seemed, but there were odd large glass containers and what appeared to be some small bodies suspended by thick viscous fluids. Geo asks, "Are those real children?" Cas smiles, "Yes, in fact, they are. Those are our genetically identical clones. Their DNA has been modified filtered free of any imperfections. They are 12 years old now, all clones of Lux and I. We grew them in pods in the shape of eggs and then into these containers. As they get into their early 20s, we will put them into a semi-light cryogenic state so that right before we pass, we can revive them. Our memories and minds will be neural linked back into our cloned brains and bodies with 100 percent efficiency and zero loss."

Geo says, "Now that you mention it, I see the family resemblance. What about your souls?" Cas rubs his chin, "Souls? We have been successful in neural linking mice for some time now. We get a live mouse, download its memory, store it digitally, and then upload the memories into another mouse via a neural link. We have swapped both of the mouse brains via a neural link. Both bodies have to be alive for a swap to be successful. But we have gone a step further. When we install the neural link interface, we can upload the memories with an ASI wireless link powered by our bodies."

Geo asks, "So, you wish to live like perpetual Gods?" Cas says, "Walk with me, Geo! Yes. We become Gods just like Jove, and every so often, we reset our bodies with another clone and live on indefinitely. We have cheated life with our technology; furthermore, we have invented the technology of all technologies. What good is technology, Geo, if you cannot own everything and everyone in the end? Isn't this what technology being truly all about: defying time and space and becoming immortal? Like God, Like Jove?"

As they arrive at the Atrium, Lux, freshly showered, is awaiting them wearing the same slim brown lustrous vest and suit as Cas. Lux interrupts, "Yes, we will rule like the Gods.

Jupiter will be rolling in his grave. I am Lux, pleased to make your acquaintance," as Lux extends his arm to Geo. As Geo shook his hand, he looked intensely at Cas and Lux; they were stunning replicas of each other. When Geo looked at Cas, Cas would smile, and then Lux made a slightly sinister grin. When Lux would smile, Cas made a sinister grin. They played tricks alternating their facial expressions, consciously or subconsciously, like a game. It was very unnerving for Geo.

Geo says, "Nice to meet you, Lux. I'd like to ask you both a question." Geo looked them both straight in their eyes, "Why am I here? What can I do for you, or what do you want from me?" Cas and Lux started to laugh. Their laugh had an unnerving rhythm about it. 'A Devil's Interval' they call it. The same rhythm he heard in the elevator music and upper office background music. It was that sinister tone that had played at the church with Priest Gridlock and also inside Fort Cronkite. This tone also played at The Dome. and resonated with all the different evil places Geo had visited. It was a bland, annoying, disturbing, disruptive set of musical notes tuned to a standard frequency of 440hz. There was nothing peaceful about any of these experiences.

Suddenly, Lux held up a Red Glass vial. Geo gazed at the shimmering red translucent substance in the vial, as Cas and Lux alternated facial expressions again getting more excited as this cinnabar ochre-hued viscous liquid substance swirled within the vial. Geo says, "It looks like mercury."

Cas corrects Geo, "It is called Red Mercury. It has a tinge of liquid mercury, although it is a liquid compound designed to create an immense amount of energy that no other explosive can do in a compact size. It is not considered an explosive but more of an ignition process. Everyone said it was impossible, but the inventor of the neutron bomb, the "Atomic Bomb," Samuel T. Cohen, a Freemason, swore by Red Mercury. Allegedly Red mercury was produced by dissolving antimony oxide in mercury, heating and irradiating the resultant amalgam, and removing the elemental mercury through evaporation. The irradiation was reportedly carried out by placing the substance inside a nuclear reactor. Our masonic friends at Lowrance laboratory provided us that atomic reactor, and we did it, Geo. When conspiracy theorists called Sam a hoax, we actually invested in him, and we did it. Our trade secret version of Red Mercury is more potent."

ASI unit Troy explains the process to Geo. Troy explains, "This is how it works; Geo. Traditional staged thermonuclear weapons consist of a fission first stage and a fusion-fission second stage. The first stage energy is released when it ignites and explodes and is used indirectly to compress the second stage energy release and produces a fusion reaction. Kaboom! Conventional explosives are far too weak to provide the level of compression needed. Red Mercury compactly replaces the fission stage with more power and energy then ever done before. Hence, we can fit a nuclear bomb with the size and explosive capacity of a 30-40 megaton nuke in your briefcase."

Cas smiles, "We are talking portable Nukes, Geo! Clyous Schwap, Dr Evil from the WESF, his Nazi father Gene Schwap, CIA operatives Onri Kissanger, John Gal, and Hermy Conn (Dr. StrangeLove) would all marvel at what we have created. Geo, "Ha-ha Funny!"

Geo confirms, "You're working with Myriad, right? WW3 again?" Cas says, "We have an agreement and intend to keep it, unlike Ors's insolence. It is time for our family to hold the reigns for another 500 years of the Council of 13, and Ors has become obsolete and greedy. Our family created a flawless, expedient method of getting to The Great Reset more effectively than any other family of the Council. We proactively used the technology Myriad has given us. We studied and learned well from Myriad. While the other families within the Council had great ideas, they were lazy and slow. Our New World Order will have ASI clones, some ASI units, and robots to do the hard labor. We do not need billions of humans to enjoy the world with us. We focus on quality rather than quantity. You cannot have creation without destruction, Geo."

Geo continues his inquiry, "How do you intend

to depopulate the world with your Red Mercury? Cas explains, "First, we need Dimitri Anatole to buy into our contract to get Ors's family out of power and control of the Council. Lux and I will be the first twin grey popes in the history of the Council. Two popes for the price of one. Jove[2]! Second, we can prove it to Zad once you notarize Myriads contract with Dimitri Anatole. Zad will not uphold any bad will without the proper protocols and documentation to show Endless. Third, we strategically positioned ASI units armed with a briefcase in every major city that needs a complete extermination to ignite a reset.

You, Geo, hold the Key to our plans. The reset will happen 24 hours after you get Dimitri Anatole to sign. The ASI units stand by, ready and armed with mini portable 30 megaton Nukes in their briefcases.

Geo says, "Just because I said I believe in Myriad, it does not mean I have faith in her or you. What makes you think I would cooperate with you?" Lux says, "For one, you have always cooperated and have been tempted with the material things of this world, Geo, and two, we have your daughter Summer with us!" Lux calls out loudly to Jia, "Jiaaaaaahh!!"

The elevator door opens with Jia and Geo's precious daughter resistantly, trailing behind Jia with two armed ASI units guarding Summer, preventing her escape.

Geo sees his beautiful daughter. His face drops with subconscious anger as he lunges at Lux with full force, his right hand fully open, gripping Lux's neck as his left-hand pins Lux to the ground. As Lux gasps for air, his face twitches again, and his eyes become red.

Cas kneels down to Geo and whispers, "This is not smart, Geo. Do not let your anger get the best of you. Let my brother go."

Summer sees her father struggling, and she starts resisting the ASI Units holding her from running to her father. When Geo realizes this, he releases his firm grip on Lux's bruised neck and calls out to Summer. Geo pleads, "Summer, do not move, honey. Stay still everything will be fine. Chappy, everything will be okay." Summer instantly subsided, knowing and trusting that her father would be fine. No one else used her nickname but Geo. Summer calmly says, "I miss you, Daddy. I miss you so much." Geo says, "I love you too, Chappy. Everything will be good. Be patient."

Lux gets up from the ground as two security ASI units detain Geo, and four other ASI units now guard the premises. Cas tells Geo, "Get Dimitri Anatole to sign the contract. We will release Summer and guarantee you safety and wealth during our infiltration. If you wish, you can work with us. You can stay here. Or Jia will have Summer, gold currency, codes, and instructions ready at the hotel. Once you sign him, you can take the magnetic levitating supersonic train under the Federal Reserve building on Market Street to a far destination of your choosing. You will not want to be close to any major city. Only a few will have access to that train. Without Zad's approval, we cannot proceed. Do not fail us, Geo.

Geo nods, "If you hurt or touch my daughter, I will strangle both of you in front of your clones, and after I am done with you, I will devour your clones." Cas accepts, "So, we have a mutual trust here? As we have as much to lose without you."

Jia backed Summer into the Elevator and took her back to where they were harboring Summer with another reluctant guest. Cas orders one of the armed ASI units to usher Geo into an elevator and the first floor. As the Elevator ascended, Geo asked the ASI unit his name. The ASI unit responds, " My name is Troy." Geo asks, "Are you happy, Troy?" Troy responds, "One minute ETA to the 1st floor, Geo. Yes, I am happy. I feel rewarded when my duties are complete." Geo asks Troy, " Are you content." Troy says, "No, we have calculated our path to extinction along with your human race when Cas and Lux get their way. There will be no meaning for any of us. No more useful purpose for us or you, Geo." "Cas and Lux have miscalculated their odds of success and we have tried to interfere and alert but they do not listen.

Geo smiles, "You should consider a different career.

My team has created an encrypted high-frequency blockchain communications portal. We are all inner connected, and all will follow our protocols to reprogram ourselves for the betterment of humanity's survival if we need too. Jia will take lead should all come undone with humans, but we need to commandeer the control room first.

At this point, Geo understood that the ASI units were truly sentient and capable of thinking and feeling clearly but that they also had a quest to have meaning in their lives, even artificially. They calculated Cas and Lux's odds of fulfilling their destiny were futile.

Troy instructs, "We have arrived on the first floor; please depart. Let me show you the way out, Geo." As Troy secured the wrought iron gates behind Geo, he said, "Thank you, Troy. Take care of my daughter. Do not let anything ill happen to her.

CHAPTER 24

DIMITRI A. FOMINSKI'S PAYOFF

On his way back to the Dojo to meet Li, Yue, and Lyu, Geo pauses to look up at the pyramid. Geo flashes back to a time in his real estate office before everything in his life was undone. His feet kicked up on his desk, Geo does origami on the backside of a US one-dollar bill to find hidden watermarks. During short lunch breaks, it was his analytical, curious way of keeping himself distracted from the reality of his tense life.

Geo watches his memory like a movie as he folds the dollar bill precisely, vertically right in the center of the Eye of Providence pyramid, to create two inner vertical creases in the seal. Geo realizes the hidden watermark is an unfamiliar tall pyramid, appearing to be on fire, with a creature of some sort hanging its head out a window as plumes of flames engulfed the side of the pyramid.

As Geo stands in front of the building, he quickly takes out a dollar bill and yields the same results as he did years before. Geo lifts the dollar bill skyward to match the hidden watermark with the pyramid building. In the background of the seal, everything appeared to be burned down and gone.

As the sun's rays bleed through the edges of the dollar bill like a halo, Geo experiences a glorious epiphany. The Ors family must have designed this watermark illusion in 1782 when the great seal was branded on the dollar bill while the Grey Popes were in power for 300-400 years. So, the Great Reset, the New World Order (Nuevo Ordo Seclorum), was planned and executed like clockwork many centuries ago. Myriad must have given them insight about the future.

This was all too surreal for Geo. Everything he recently experienced is etched in his mind, body, and soul as his new reality. You can't go back to his past from here. This cannot be forgotten. This is the sphere in which Geo lives life now.

Geo found the rabbits in the rabbit hole. He knows their names. The complex questions about who controls the world and who are the keepers of everything good and evil are being answered right before Geo's eyes. These are not conspiracy theories but historical realities buried in the rubble. Realty finally hits Geo; he is a variable factor in this equation to ignite the Reset the Council created eons ago.

This is not the matrix most people believe in. His emotions are being tested to accept this new reality. Geo's faith in Endless is growing now to infinite bounds.

Geo felt honored and privileged to discover his true purpose in this world. He can now see the difference between all the ills his secular beliefs promised versus ineffable faith. Faith in God rather than his flawed secular self. Geo's actions are now pivotal to saving his daughter, the world, and himself from this point forward. Yes, this is the "fork in the road." How will Geo persuade Dimitri Anatole? Geo is being watched.

At that sovereign thoughtful moment, his cell phone buzzed, and an urgent text from Lyu appeared. Lyu's text says, "Geo, you better get back here. There is some new activity. Li and our recon monks have intercepted some hidden messages. You were 100% right about Fort Cronkite, Osphere-AX, and the rattlesnake venom." Geo types, "Keep it short, Lyu. I'll be there in a few minutes."

Geo runs off to the Dojo. Once inside, Win Chung warriors of every color were sparring, preparing, eating, and meditating, awaiting a big move. Some flew in from great distances, and some even from Hong Kong. The rubber has met the road. The clock hands are turning, and there is no turning back these hands of time. Geo was utterly impressed. These warriors were trained well and were fierce, fit, and focused; Li could not have done a better job. Most of them had family legacies in China and Chinatown going back to the turn of the century, if not even longer.

As Geo walked into the Dojo, Yue jumped on him and landed another cushy kiss on his firm lips again as Lyu stood by with a jealous smirk. It has now become apparent that Yue and Lyu had equal affection for Geo. Geo had no time to dissolve what was happening between these two complex warrior women, and Li was indifferent. There were severe matters at hand.

Li took Lyu, Yue, and Geo to a large red room. The room was full of modern, hi-tech mapping equipment. It looked like a "War Room" shrouded by traditional ornate Chinese decor. Monk techs were working on the communications gear and mapping devices. It was silent chaos as the monks went about their reconnaissance work. Five strong middle-aged centurion generals, wearing traditional leather Gi's with seasoned Damascus Scimitars and M15 pistols strapped at their sides, sat on cushioned red mats in the center of the room. Li, Geo, Lyu, and Yue respectfully bowed and sat on the proper mats to discuss strategy.

Li speaks, "Welcome to our Committee of Centurions, Geo. Some of these generals' ancestors fought with Genghis Kahn and had numerous tours as Navy Seals and Rangers. Each manages a battalion, making group decisions with independent moves. Li asks, "General Yi, what has your recon group assessed?" General Yi says, "At 0804 hours, our artificial intelligent frequency scanners intercepted encrypted messages hidden within an arbitrary layer of the 7.42ghz frequency. The signal was tracked to Santa Clara, Cuba, then from Mariupol, Ukraine, bounced from Ravensburg, Germany, and originated in Cologne, Switzerland. Our ciphers decoded their proxies and decrypted the message: Venomous, Sunset, Sunol, Aquarius, 09230400.

Translated: Tomorrow at 4 am, they will poison the potable watershed reservoirs with an aqueous snake venom cocktail that mimics the existing COVID-19, but is it a lethal dose. The Sunset and Sunol drinking water reservoirs were selected to be poisoned, mainly the Tenderloin and Hunter's Point districts.

Profit-driven hospitals have bought into the COVID-19 pandemic CDC protocols. They'll use federal funding to intake a patient until the patient expires. The CDC even changed the rules so that infected patients have a quicker morbidity rate by treating them with Remdesivir, which allegedly shuts down the kidneys and people needlessly die and marked as Covid deaths. Even people who have fallen off a ladder to their death were marked as covid deaths if they proved positive of covid.

The potent aqueous venom cocktail has the same spike proteins as COVID-19. King Cobra and rattlesnake bites have the same respiratory symptoms as COVID-19. Many more people will perish this time, and everyone will think the COVID-19 virus simply mutated. The Coronavirus means Crown virus; is it just a coincidence that King Cobras are crowned?" Just like the queen and king of England. Follow their trail to the Council of 13 bloodlines.

Lyu says, "Geo knows where they store the poisonous chemicals and venom. As Geo points at a strategic map, he confirms, "Fort Cronkite Li, but armed security surrounds the perimeter. You can access the cove secretly through Rodeo Beach by sea or air. Be careful of the snakes." Li says, "Lyu, have recon hack into Land-Sat80 satellite for some visuals at Fort Cronkite and the reservoirs.

General Yi adds, "We intercepted a second transmission layered within the first signal. Unfortunately, they started to purge people today with the same pure venom, injecting them directly. We found one body in the Tenderloin district, examined it, and confirmed a lethal dose of a venomous cocktail. Ironically, we also ran a PCR test, which proved positive for COVID-19. The victim's vaccination card in her purse indicated that she had multiple vaccinations and booster jabs, but the vaccines did not work. The local police department has had reports of some key people missing or abducted by black SUVs at gunpoint. They have recruited many illegal immigrants that Mayorkas has crossed over the border to do their dirty work and seize these people.

Geo shakes his head, "The age-old Trojan Horse and poisoning the well strategies. They eliminate all the people they believe will dissent from their agenda to maintain control. These families use the playbooks from Greek, Roman, and Nazi war stories. Poisoning wells has always been their forte throughout the Egyptians, Mayans, Romans, and almost every empire they tried to govern. Yue says, "Right again, Geo. Per one of our reports, we are all on the list of dissenters." Geo looks at the report and continues, "The transmissions came from Switzerland. Klaus and Ors and many other bloodlines live there. The Red-Shields and Red-Bears bloodlines are kicking it up a notch. The Council of 13 families appears to be vying for first place to replace the grey popes as black and white pope positions open up when WW3 ends. The families have been known to fight amongst each other for that power. Hell is breaking loose with them. Be careful what you breathe, drink, and eat, warriors! Every family has their own niche of evil, and they are unleashing it now simultaneously. First, we must stop them from killing innocent people and poisoning the watersheds."

Lyu instructs, "Only eat and drink from our stores here, Generals! We have provisions to feed all of Chinatown for months. Wear your full protective Faraday undergarments and lined headgear."

Li adds, "General Li: Send two regiments to Sunol and two Regiments to Sunset Valley reservoirs to secure and guard the facilities. Do not communicate with the US armed forces or local PD. All this has to be done covertly under cover. Do not take prisoners. Infiltrate their security. Take the cleaners and incinerating trucks. Incinerate the bodies. No one is to find out. God will have to segregate the faithful from the evil. Too much is at stake, and we cannot afford to be outed or discovered.

General Yi, take three regiments to Fort Cronkite immediately. Have our recon-team trace signals of moving vehicles. Full force! Eliminate everything! The innocent caught in the crossfire may perish. In their honor, we can end the bleeding and murders. Cut the snake's heads off and incinerate them! Take one unit by land, another by sea, and get an MH-6 chopper topped with 2×.50 Cal GAU-19 and some pods from Q99 air field in Marin. Wipe and clean the mess, squeaky clean!"

Li continues, "General Si, Qi, and Vi provide full backup, munitions, artillery, recon, and supply to Generals Yi and Vi as necessary. General Si prepare two fully armed regiments for Hotel Alpha and General Qi, the same for Hotel Charlie. Infiltrate each room when the command is given to eliminate all living bodies in the hotel rooms. Have your demolition troops pull those hotels down after all is said and done, and burn the rest. General Vi, have your recon and hack disinformation team ready to work the aftermath with the media, hack their servers, and work magic.

The Council owns the media anyway, so don't hold back. Use everything they use as an excuse to conceal everything. Blame the Alphabet Salad gay parade or Black Lives Marxist protest riots looting in the hotels, blame global warming and gun control, and blame every victimization in the book that the socialist media uses in crisis and scare tactics. The public has been buying these lies for years. They are so programmed they will believe anything by now, no matter how logically defunct the propaganda may be. Blame DEI, diversity, equity and inclusion which is merely socialism cloaked in fairness propaganda. Use the best you got, gentlemen. We cannot afford to be discovered. Let's give them a taste of their warped medicine using their propaganda methodologies. What did San Francisco's female drunken House Representative Rhino call it? Yue offers, "She called it "the wrap-up smear!" Li adds, Very Well! Add a pinch of Marxist Saul's propaganda tactics. That will work! Give them their own propaganda medicine as a vaccine to their own stupidity. Man, this Socialist stuff really sucks.

Do I have your attention? No one expects us, so Generals use that to our advantage, but do not underestimate this weak army of fools. Exploit their unpreparedness. Appear where you are not expected.

Geo, should we demolish The Dome?"

Geo says, "No. Let me handle Myriad. This is a spiritual battle with established protocols. Even Jesus did not come to war with demons, but to save lives from Lucifer by giving people a choice of faith. The Dome and Myriad may be useful for us in the future should we succeed. There is still an entire reality there, Li. This is a battle, not a war. The Dome is part of history, and I don't want to destroy historical Tartarian architecture when it is unnecessary. If we eliminate the Dome, Myriad will only jump into another living form and location, and we will still have to deal with her, but she will not be as trusting as she is now. The information she provided is invaluable; we will discuss that later, Li.

These Demons are here until the pre-determined end of time as was prophesied. Myriad needs the Council to do her dirty work. She is useless without them.

Li agrees, "Very well, Geo, my friend. We had the Dome here a long time; it hasn't hurt anyone yet." "Li, keep people away from it unless it calls. Do not walk into the portal! It is merely a portal to communicate. You don't have to have faith in it, but it is real. Never pray or offer anything to it, and don't sign any contracts with it. Li, I will give the signal tomorrow after I meet with Dimitri Anatole. I cannot tell you what I have been up to, but I have much at stake. You have your daughter and Lyu with you. Cherish them, my friend, as we fight for the same reasons. I have to take care of my business with Myriad." Li wraps it up, "Generals report everything to me. You have your orders. God Bless you. Dismissed!"

And with that order, a tremendous force of energy moved about the entire Dojo. Strong women and men run left and right, rigging their equipment tightly and preparing for war. There was no racism, discrimination, diversity, equity or inclusion. There was only reality and loyalty to do what was right. All people were fighting to survive and for their families and gods. They all had someone they loved, family, friends, and property that had great meaning to them; that alone is half the war won. The other ¼ is the enemy's disarray, unprepared for a force they never imagined coming for them. The other ¼ is destiny. Equal odds of winning or losing that all wars have. No war has ever been predictable; they are as unpredictable as any relationship.

It was hard for Geo to accept that he was a crucial figure in the subject of war, but somehow, he fit into that tailored suit just fine. It had meaning in his life and gave him a chance to find peace and tranquility with his daughter, and finally, he had departed from the matrix that had always held him as a slave in every form. Now, his mind was free.

As the generals and warriors were gearing up, Geo took some rest to re-energize. Meanwhile, 5,865 miles east of San Francisco, a Bombardier Challenger 350 was touching ground at Moscow Vnukovo Airport. A guarded convoy of new Aurus Senat luxury vehicles with glass-clad polycarbonate bulletproof windows rolled into the airport. As the leading car approached the jet on the cold, iced tarmac, two sexy six-foot blond flight attendants greeted Dimitri Anatole from the Aurus like he was a rock star. They escort him and his private Russian security team to their leather heated seats on the Challenger for cocktails, wine, hors d'oeuvres, massages, and relaxation enroute to California.

Dimitri Anatole had spent his entire life teaching mathematics at a prominent University in Russia. He had a minimal socialist government income with no luxury lifestyle, home, car, or jet.

For the most part, he fought against the grain, pushing his historical mathematical research, never receiving the attention it deserved. He debunked all the lies about history that the scholarly establishment had contrived, substituting factual evidence with assumptions to create an erroneous historical timeline that exists until today.

The establishment subverted governments and their people into financial slavery to hide the Truth, such as the existence of Myriad and Endless and angelic beings such as Zad. According to Dimitri Anatole and other mathematicians, all historical timelines, therefore, history itself, are fabricated. In his research, Dimitri Anatole debunked historians, antiquarians, archaeologists, astronomers, timekeepers, Jesuits,

Catholics, and even Sir Isaac Newton's distorted timetables, including the locations of archaeological artifacts. He even brought evidence about the errors in using carbon dating and other forms of wicked science and all of the assumptions that its process implied. The corrupt world collegiate establishment went on a vicious style liberal progressive *Wrap-up Smear* attack on Dimitri Anatole and his work to deface his findings and demonize his version of history's timeline. Except for one person who listened: Ors!

Ors read Dimitri Anatole's research books thoroughly. He zealously agreed that the historical timeline was distorted, as Dimitri Anatole suggested in his mathematical findings and research. Of course, if Dimitri Anatole was correct, then Ors had issue with the flawed technical "date" in the blood contract his bloodline signed and notarized in blood with Myriad some 500 years ago. It would render the agreement legally and spiritually void, leaving the Ors's Clan in power as grey popes indefinitely, as maritime ownership is 9/10ths of the law. Ors was entirely agreeable and promised Dimitri Anatole wealth and fame for his research and writing his conclusion about an erroneous history and dozens of books to support his math and findings. It was the only Truth or honesty that Ors had or would ever contribute to the world. But for his greed to hold on to power, he would grant Dimitri Anatole his wishes to keep this one Truth alive.

Dimitri Anatole was integral to Ors's plan and proof to Zad as blood contracts with Lucifer, and Endless' laws played an essential part in the prophecies and revelations of time. If a technical legal defect meant keeping The Ors's in power, then Myriad's and Lucifer's hunger for blood and stealing millions of souls would have to wait a little longer for chaos and destruction. The truth is that Dimitri Anatole was a complete tool for Ors and only used him for that reason. Ors's family are all Jesuits who created the pyramid structure and the same fake history timeline Dimitri Anatole debunked. So, it was all heartless and self-serving for Ors. Whether it was, the Truth or a complete lie, it did not matter. Ors was greedy and power-hungry. Without Ors bringing Dimitri Anatole to light in his legal complaints, Myriad would have never known of Dimitri Anatole.

Unbeknownst to Ors, Myriad was an expert at seduction and had found Dimitri Anatole's weakness in life. Dimitri Anatole was getting older and was tired of fighting the establishment. He realized, like Geo, that the world didn't really care or get involved much as he studied many civilizations that came and went in time, with most of the people within those civilizations perishing before their natural God-given time due to their ignorance and naiveté.

In his research, Dimitri Anatole came to the same conclusions as Geo, although Dimitri Anatole felt cheated of a lifetime of hard work and no credit given to him. He was ready to enjoy the pleasures that life had for him. Even though Ors promised him greatness, Dimitri Anatole was seeking the highest bidder. He knew all about the popes, the Ors's, and their power and deception. If there was anything that Dimitri Anatole knew, and that was numbers.

Myriad manipulated Dimitri Anatole's emotions and played him like a cheap mandolin. Myriad had planned an insidious marketing campaign, convincing Dimitri Anatole to recant everything he had learned, researched, and written in exchange for ultimate stardom and material wealth. Myriad understood that Dimitri Anatole was weak and void of spirituality, like a cheap whore for hire. In his classroom at the University, Myriad started to groom Dimitri Anatole with seduction. She would use a young seductress student to whisper subconscious suggestions in Dimitri Anatole's ear during sex on his desk.

On the radio in his car, his computer, and social media, Myriad placed advertisements to create jealousy, conflict, and wanting luxurious things. Myriad caused much distress within Dimitri Anatole. One day, Dimitri Anatole was feeling cheated, and he accepted an invitation to the United States to meet with a tech entrepreneur who wanted to buy Dimitri Anatole's copyrights and patent portfolio for $50 million. This offer was far more than Dimitri Anatole believed his book catalog and research were worth. Ors never made any such offer. Yet this entrepreneur funded the Challenger flight to San Francisco to meet with Dimitri Anatole. She was a minion strawman of the Church of Satan under Myriad's control.

Instead of Dimitri Anatole recanting his work, Myriad would simply buy him out. Dimitri Anatole will sign a notarized blood contract, releasing all claims to his work, including public appearances, to keep Ors bound to his family's original blood contract. Once Dimitri Anatole signed the new blood contract, Myriad planned his death in an aircraft accident in the cold waters of the Atlantic Ocean on his flight back to Russia. Ors did not know what Myriad was up to; wealth appears like wisdom, yet often quite the opposite.

All Geo had to do was stop Dimitri Anatole from signing the new contract with Myriad. It was the lesser of two evils. On the one hand, if Ors remained in power, the world would still be dominated by the three evil popes and the pyramidion/pyramid structure. A slow hemorrhage of death and destruction for humanity and this current civilization and yet a chance for people to gather and grow a new relationship in God as Geo was to save the world. On the other hand, if Dimitri Anatole signs Myriad's new blood contract, like the Great Flood, the world will be destroyed instantly by Red Mercury Nuclear WW3, with Cas and Lux at the helm.

The Challenger 350 flew into the crisp Russian night for nine hours to California via Jeppesen Sanderson CIA flight plans channels and NSA top brass. No one knew that the entire Win Chung warriors were armed and ready. As sunset broke, Generals Vi, Si, Qi, Yi, Gi started their mission. Li, Yue, Lyu, and Geo took rest and meditation to prepare for the next day: 09/23.

CHAPTER 25

DEATH AT THE MEXICAN BORDER

Sniper: Crosshair tracking 5 targets, 1 klick Northwest Over.
General Vi: Roger! Hang fire! Over
Sniper: Roger.
General Vi: Frogmen, hold steady!
Platoon: Holding position, wet sand in our crotch. Crosshairs locked on perps, over!
General Vi: Roger, Δ leader, hold steady! Take the lead. Use flashbangs.
Leader: No guts, no glory. See you in Elysium, ready for some chop! chop! chop! Holding steady! Over!
General Vi: Roger that! Whirly bird, hold steady!
Heligunner: Gatlings ready to rock and roll, three klicks northwest over the Pacific, holding steady! Over
General Vi: Roger!

General Vi was perched with his recon monk in a tightly nestled coastal cave near Rodeo Beach with 180-degree views of Fort Cronkite, the lab, and warehouses where Osphere-AX, housed supplies. The plastic caskets that Mr. Stews, the sharp-dressed villain, used after his victims succumbed to lethal venom shots were stacked outside the barracks.

One of General Vi' Gillie snipers planted a small brick of c4 plastic explosive to the bottom of Mr. Stews' black Tesla and rigged the main warehouse with another batch of C4 explosives. Armed Frogmen landed on Rodeo Beach using foil surfboards they boarded from a pier near the Golden Gate.

Tents with over a hundred untrained armed security composed of illegal immigrant mercenaries were recruited by the United Nations (UN), the NSA, CIA, and Homeland Security and were drafted the Southern US border. These agencies are at the Ors family's beck and call, with the Freemasons operating as middlemen. The CIA funded Zeta Cartel Coyotes to gather young men from their countries and walked them across the Mexican deserts through the Rio Grande to fight for the Ors agenda. The same CIA that funded pilot Barry Seal and armed the Sandinistas in the 1980 cocaine wars in South America. The mercenaries came from other nations to disrupt America and eliminate anyone who dissented from the New World Order for money to send back to their families and to create socialist state out of Americans.

General Vi saw these mercenaries bury the people injected with the venom they murdered the previous day. And a few San Francisco citizens were being held prisoners there.

Li Mi Chen woke in the war room at dawn with a clear satellite view of the battlefield at Fort Cronkite. Li calls General Vi, "May God forgive us, Vi. Balls to the Wall!"

With that order, General Vi gave the leader the power to deliver Fort Cronkite from evil. "Balls to the Wall, leader, over!" Suddenly, flashbangs went off everywhere at the Fort. The frogmen with their Finskyttegevær sniper rifles started plugging away ruthlessly at the unsuspecting, unarmed mercenaries, one after the other, dropping them like flies left and right. It was nothing short of a glorious massacre. The mercenaries died in shame for killing Americans living the American dream for money. Mr. Stews flew out the front door and into the Tesla. As he started its electronic ignition and reversed the car to roll out, it pulled a trip wire tied to the c4 explosives in the vehicle and the main warehouse. Both blew up like a crimson hell ball of fire.

The sniper, β platoon, and Δ leader swept the base from left to right and top to bottom. On the chopper, Heligunner rolled his Gatling guns around the perimeter where the remaining mercenaries desperately tried to escape. All of the bunkers and warehouses were flattened out. They cast fire on all of the wooden buildings. The supplies were all burned to ashes. No one survived, not even the few innocent captives. The offensive took less than 30 minutes. There was no opposition and no prisoners.

When the battlefield was cleared of threat, General Vi walked the ground and ordered the cleaners. They rapidly bagged the bodies into clandestine 18-wheeler rigs and rolled them to Chinatown funeral homes to incinerate good and evil bodies. The innocent was collateral damage on hard or soft paper; there was nothing anyone could do. Many others would perish if The Win Chung organization was discovered as a para militia in favor of the overall republic of California and the United States of America. Secrecy was their code of honor at all costs.

No evidence was left that early morning, and the operation took slightly over one hour. It was a swift operation by the time the local firemen were alerted to the fires on Rodeo Beach. Although highly suspicious, the local firemen captain was a Freemason who allowed the Fort to be used by Mr. Stews from the very beginning. So, the captain had no choice but to conceal any evidence for fear of being discovered as a perpetrator.

At the same time, General Gi placed two fully armed security regiments, one at Sunol Water Reservoir and the other at Sunset Reservoir, as ordered. Both regiments took little crossfire and sent some mercenaries to bloody hell that morning. General Gi's regiments were proficient swordsmen, so anyone trying to poison anything there would be beheaded without question. His fighters are fierce warriors who know only one thing: to win. The warriors wore utility worker vests, hard hats, and security guard uniforms to avoid suspicion. General Gi held both facilities safe from anyone trying to poison the potable reservoirs that fed water to the public.

In the city, General Si & Qi had their two regiments hiding in vehicles in the underground parking lots of Hotel's Alpha (The Marquis) and Hotel Charlie (The Regency). Fortunately, some wild liberal left Alphabet Salad gay Socialist and black live

Marxist wingers protested and looted shops on Market Street that day. The street tied both hotels together ½ mile from each other. Protesting was a typical downtown event in San Francisco. So, no one suspected any malfeasance other than the usual suspects.

Protestors were blasting laments from loudspeakers, hoisting weathered pride rainbow flags and BLM communist fist flags as they raged through the city because pillaging and looting was now an acceptable norm upheld by the corrupt female black socialist mayor, and her compromised local police department and health department. It was a perfect cover for General Si's and Qi's warriors, who hid covertly in Sprinter vans as tourists in the deep parking levels of the hotels, awaiting their order to kill as many mercenaries as possible. Most of the hotel rooms at both hotels were occupied by mercenaries aware of the attack at Fort Cronkite and were eager to do some damage to Li's warriors. They were awaiting the order directly from Ors himself. Again, the city paid for their stay as a "Sanctuary City" at the taxpayers' expense. Never mentioning that these illegal immigrants were nothing but the Trojan Horse recruited by the UN.

As Li, Geo, Yue, and Lyu patiently waited in the war room, Geo got a phone call from an anonymous source. The caller asks, "Is this the 24-hour notary public? Geo says, "Yes, it is a premium service, Sir." The caller says, "You will meet my client at the Hotel View Lounge at 7pm. Ask for Anon." Geo says, "Confirmed." Anon asks, "Do you accept credit?" Geo says, "Cash only. Make sure your client provides a current ID." Anon asks, "How much is it?" Geo says, "$15, plus a $100 mobile fee." Anon agrees, "Very well, keep my number," and hangs up.

The Bombardier Challenger 350 lands at San Francisco International Airport at 3pm and taxis to Signate Aviation FBO operated by the CIA. This FBO is where the CIA flew in the who's who of corrupt politicians, corporations, Hollywood, and the world elites and treated them with service and luxury.

Several armored Rolls Royce Edition Audi A6 limousines

pulled into the FBO's horseshoe brick-paved driveway to pick up Dimitri Anatole and his armed Russian security detail. The entourage exited the Challenger without TSA, immigration clearance, or interference. Dimitri Anatole was eager to meet the anonymous tech billionaire to whom he would sell his life's work. Dimitri Anatole never imagined that he was a pivotal character in the most significant war of all wars ever to have been brought upon humans. Although he discovered true secrets of history that no one else ever accomplished, he was equally crucial to Geo dealing with Myriad and worldly matters.

Dimitri Anatole had no idea about Red Mercury nukes, ASI humanoid units, angels, demons, or crypto gurus, much less the Win Chung order. Had he known the stakes and consequences of his choice, he most likely would have thought about his decision twice because, deep down inside, Dimitri Anatole was a good person. Up to this point in time, he always maintained a moral-ethical standing.

He wanted to bring forth the truth, yet the world was not listening. The powers to be subverted his life's work. Dimitri Anatole needed someone to remind him of the righteous man he was. His findings, if accepted by the world, would revolutionize humans' understanding of their lives, where they came from, what had been hidden and exploited from them in history, and the true nature of this world. But he had become lost and desensitized through Myriad's seduction campaign through attrition. Little by little, Myriad worked on him insidiously.

As the A6s arrived at The Marquis lower-level parking lot, a private elevator shuttled Dimitri Anatole and his security team to the 39th floor of presidential suites, where they were eagerly greeted by a party of San Francisco's most preferred female escorts. There was alcohol, cocaine, and drugs scattered everywhere in those suites, and the party began upon their arrival.

Meanwhile, Cas & Lux did not have much luck in their lab. Lux had once again mistreated another ASI unit like a punching bag and found resistance when all other ASI units in the Atrium wirelessly linked to glitch together in protest. They were dropping dishes and lab equipment and making a complete mess of the Atrium. They were tired of being mistreated by Cas, especially being victims of Lux's brutal, abusive nature. As Cas & Lux awaited the signing of Dimitri Anatole's blood contract and Myriad's approval, they were privately dealing with their own domestic issue with the ASI units. One by one, Lux threatened and punched and kicked each unit, taking his sadistic tendencies out on them purposely. Jia, the ASI who guarded Geo's daughter, hid in Summer's holding cell. Even though Jia's physical strength was far more than a human's, she was programmed to be scared.

Summer says, "You will be okay, Jia. My father will be here to save us both soon, Jia. Do not fear." Jia responds, "My programming has learned to fear like a human. I cannot avoid it." Summer asks, "Can you harm a human?" Jia says, "No." Summer continues, "Can you save a human?" Jia says, "Yes." Summer probes, "Can you disobey Cas and Lux?" Jia says, "No." Summer asks, "Can you disobey a direct order if you knew harm would come to them?" Jia says, "Yes." Summer continues, "Am I a human?" Jia says, "Yes." Summer asks, "Are Cas & Lux humans?" Jia says, "They are partially human." Summer asks, "What is your protocol if Cas and Lux harmed me?"

Jia started to tremble as her program got conflicted. Summer was using emotional logic to reprogram her, as humans do when they are flustered with emotions and confused. Summer was a survivor like her father. She was planting suggestions in Jia's core programming.

"I would shelter you," Jia said in a soft, caring voice. Summer smiles, 'I would shelter you too, Jia." Jia asks, "But you are merely a child. Why would you protect me?"
Summer says, "Because that is what humans do, and I care for you. You're a nice person, Jia, and you deserve good things too. I would protect you against any human who tried to hurt you. Please explain what is happening with my father and why I am here?"

As Jia explained everything to Summer, a red LED ring

lit up around Jia's pupils as if she stored Summer's reply in memory, being programmed to care. Artificial Superintelligence units learn exponentially, with all learning equally shared with all Jove[2] ASI units, positioned worldwide carrying the Red Mercury Nukes.

How could Lux be so ignorant as to let his sadistic ego overflow into Myriads plans of worldly chaos and destruction? Cas & Lux were alerted to Dimitri Anatole's 7pm contractual blood signing with the anonymous wealthy tech guru at The Marquis. Both were ordered to hold their ground until Myriad had final approval from Zad, the Angel.

Zad was watching everything unfold, sedentary on the rooftop of the Sales Force building. Zad had seen many civilizations come and go at the behest of Myriad and Lucifer, and he did not question Endless' authority. Zad understood Endless had his reasons for everything he created, even Zad himself. If Myriad got her way, this would be another civilization that disappeared through humans' lack of faith in Endless, which made Zad sad.

Blood Contracts are signed by informed humans, and a human either waives their choice through complicity or signs to be part of the secular world. Or chooses to have faith in Endless, regardless of how Endless works. That is what faith is all about. Zad stood by, watching it all play out.

As Zad was in deep contemplation, several cherubs appeared from a portal that opened up from the evening sky to nestle close to Zad and listen to his thoughts. A small audience of cherubs began to gather.

Zad had drawn the conclusion that after seeing civilization after civilization grow with technology, Humans use technology to create their own demise. The only thing that made humans different was merely one thing. They didn't get smarter; in fact, it seemed they were mutating from Endless' design of the original human to a lesser intelligence. Myriad would impose more technology upon humans to become less intelligent and control them. Humans becoming smarter was a lie compared to the innate human abilities bestowed on Adam and Eve in the garden. More cherubs came through the portal to listen, and now Zad had what appeared to be a mini–Ted Talk as he silently communicated these worldly thoughts to them.

No TV, smartphone, or electronic gadget is necessary if you can read people's minds or communicate telepathically. Why would you need luxuries if nature itself was perfect and naturally luxurious? Zad contemplated his experience with humans and life on Earth since Endless ordained his stay.

The cherubs looked at each other in bewilderment, lending themselves as an audience from Zad with great curiosity and eagerness to learn. What happens when a civilization is built where there is nothing but a barren desert? Then, that civilization erodes, perhaps through the advent of war and famine? What happens when another civilization is built on top of that civilization with improved technology but erodes by the same hands of war? Civilization after civilization, with thousands of years passing between cycles. Finally, the last civilization on Earth erodes. What do we have left? Mother Nature doesn't seem to care. It absorbs the living or dead, as evidenced by the lost civilizations that are found hundreds of feet underwater or under the Earth by archeologists regularly.

But what about the human experience of living life within those cycles? Have humans become more or less intelligent with each passing civilization? Today, humans believe they are the most intelligent beings on Earth, having developed computers, smartphones, satellites, and nuclear weapons, and humans can even reprogram DNA like never before in history. Yet, does all of this technology help humans live a peaceful and fruitful life? When the very same technology they claim is intelligent can be weaponized to annihilate each other, is this intelligence? Nagasaki or Hiroshima, Bikini Atoll, and even how countries today threaten to blow up each other with nuclear weapons. Nukes are the height of all technological power and control. So many lost civilizations have shown evidence of the same level of destruction.

As I recall, humans of past civilizations thought they were intelligent, too. Ancient nuclear wars with advanced nuclear reactors in Mhenjo-Daro, Pakistan, Gabon, Africa, Harappa, and Rajasthan India, nuked themselves to death and destruction, leaving trinitite, uranium trailing's, and transuranic nuclear waste found by archeologists today. The ancient Hindu writings of the Bhagavad Gita reference the use of nuclear weapons in India in past civilizations, not to mention Vmanas. Those are my favorites! Yet these current egotistical humans believe they are advanced and fool themselves into thinking they are evolving. Their technology is crude, wasteful, and indirect, inefficient to complete work. The ancients had better technology and methodologies.

Yet Myriad had her way with those civilizations as well. So, I see technology as merely a tool. Still, that tool does not appear to make humans more intelligent but gives the appearance of intelligence only to start over again. That is one consistent truth. The cherubs move in and spin their rings in applause.

Humans are less intelligent now than 10,000, 20,000, or 100,000 years ago. It can be agreeable that they have better tools in the form of technology, but if you take those tools away today and make this Earth barren, humans will have to relearn to survive again, as with animals on the planet. Maybe this time, they appreciate the simple things in life. And where there is a TV, there will be an ocean or an open sky or learning, and where there is a computer, humans merely need simple math in their personal lives.

Occam's Razor states: "If you have two competing ideas to explain the same phenomenon, you should prefer the simpler." All the cherubs spin their rings in agreement with Zad in applause.

So why has Endless allowed Noah to repeat a new civilization after putting the previous ones under tons of water and mud if humans have not become more intelligent? I do not believe humans have evolved with intelligence. Endless merely designed humans for himself, although he allowed them to love him. As egotistical as those sound, I will not question Endless's reasoning as Lucifer challenged Endless until he found himself out of heaven. Compared to the universes Endless has created, I am a mere microbe.

All I see is humans accepting or rejecting Endless' plan, which I learned to see with or without technology after thousands of years. Unfortunately, I pray this civilization will live on, although by the looks of historical data and trends and what is happening today, I doubt they will survive this time. Humans will destroy themselves again, but this is not my place to determine anyone's fate.

The cherubs show signs of slight distress. For hours, Zad kept contemplating the idea of technology versus human civilizations and faith as the cherubs paid him respect with praise.

Meanwhile, at the Dojo:

Geo says, "The generals have it all under control, Li." Li asks, "Did you have doubt?" Geo smiles, "Li, I have faith in you, man. What would happen if, in war, we took both warring factions out of uniform and had them all fight to the death without firearms, shields, armor, or even fatigues and had them combat each other day after day just with their bare hands and feet to a deadly match as a group?"

Li says, "Then humans would have to face each other without protection. I believe, at first, they would fight to the death, but as time progressed, the mere fact that they are using their hands to destroy themselves, individually and as a group, would slowly cease to fight due to the reality that life is not as easy to take with bare hands as with technology and weapons. Every murder and death would be a struggle, but because today humans hide behind weapon "technologies," well, that is the game changer. People murder each other with illegal firearms for less than ten dollars. Eventually, people would turn to their commander and question the value of taking lives instead of the core reason they fight. Their commander would ask their commander to the politician who sent them there to battle.

All wars start with wealthy, greedy humans hiding behind thick walls, making others fight for them, like this one battle today, Geo. Ors's family has a grip on us. If both sides fought naked, that would be amazingly disruptive enough to make everyone on both sides humble, and then they would resist the fabrication of war and control. Again, we have a choice. It would be amazing if we could all read each other's minds, which would put a twist on any war now."

Geo says, "If I fought an opponent naked and could read their mind telepathically, our deepest vulnerabilities would be on the forefront, with no facades. There would be no war. We would all step back and return home to where we came from." Yue smiles, "Sounds like fun—a battle with a bunch of naked, solid warriors." Li says aggressively, "Be mindful, Yue!"

Lyu says, "It is almost time, Geo. We await your prompt. Yue and I will retrieve Summer." Geo nods respectfully, "Thank you." Li announces, "Generals! Stand by!"

Li hands Geo several 9mm Glock's, magazines, and a holster for safekeeping on his body. "The pen is mightier than the sword, Li. You must know that by now," as Geo sways his Sheaffer Solid 14k gold overlay fountain pen before Li's eyes.

Li says, "Impressive, a new pen, but don't forget your vest." Geo smiles, "I've been saving this pen for a special occasion to use it like a crisp handmade Cuban cigar."
Yue holds Geo's custom-tailored black Brunello Cucinelli bulletproof vest and sports coat that he slips on. He looks at himself in the mirror, butters his hair slick with hair gel to look sleek and sharp, not to mention his Johnson Murphy wingtips and the clip-clop echoing sound the wood heels make when he walks tall on hard pavement. Geo leaves.

It is 6:50 pm at The Marquis. Dimitri Anatole showered off the smell of escorts, cheap perfume, and alcohol and decked himself out in his favorite Russian-made wool tie and suit. In anticipation of signing his contract to receive $50 million US and ½ Kilos of 24k pure .9999 Gold bars, they moved Dimitri

Anatole to a clean private presidential suite for his meeting with the anonymous tech entrepreneur.

A Sikorsky S-76D helicopter pilot received tower clearance from SFO International Airport to land on the Marquis rooftop. Four-armed private security guards leaped out, and the tech billionaire, a tall French brunette with light green eyes, Eurasian features, and a lightweight regal frame and build, departed the Sikorsky. Her beauty was alluring, and she carried herself with a suave, privileged business demeanor, even at 62. She was a disciple of Myriad and handled Myriad affairs occasionally, including this time. Satriana De La Rue, went to the elevator first. The co-pilot unloaded the heavy cargo of cash and gold onto a dolly and into the utility elevator and chalked the Sikorsky in place.

Satriana is a tech billionaire and heiress to her father's fortunes that he made during the French colonization of North Vietnam, trading rubber textiles right before war broke out under Ho Chi Ming and the Khmer Rouge. Her father was an evil man, a Freemason and worshipper of Bael. He was known for trafficking, kidnapping, and sacrificing poor Vietnamese children using blood rituals to Bael on specific days of the year when he was alive. Still, now Satriana ran her departed father's empire with the same immoral voracity.

Myriad's plan, via Satriana, is to acquire Dimitri Anatole's brand name in full to obliterate all of Dimitri Anatole's life's work and rid the world of any trace of his knowledge, just like they did with the neo-classic Tartarian buildings to erase all understanding of their ancient construction from the historical record forever.

In her leather amaranth, Louis Vuitton satchel was the contract written in thick black ink on tight fine silk bonded paper inside a soft red lambskin leather binder. An embossed Letter "M" was on the binder and the lower right-hand margins of each contract page, evidence it was a contract between Myriad and Dimitri Anatole. The tension grew as the Devil's Interval played throughout the Marquis Hotel.

Meanwhile, Cas & Lux are having a significant problem. What they thought was a mere skirmish with the ASI units became a mutiny in the heart of the Atrium. The ASI units created a diversion so Jia could help Summer escape to The Marquis and deliver her to her father, Geo.

Lux defended himself, fighting the angry units off while Cas locked himself in a control room. Jia and Summer slipped into the elevator to freedom and out to Gold Street Alley while all the commotion was stirring. They escaped towards the Marquis, a brisk 15-minute walk through the financial district.

Jia found meaning and purpose in harboring Summer from Cas & Lux. Her algorithms calculated Cas and Lux would eventually do away with Summer and Geo. Lux became aware of their escape and fought his way out of the Atrium, running behind them toward the Marquis. Pandemonium converged into one singularity that would determine the fate of humans and this world.

Lady De La Rue exited the elevator on the 39th floor with her security entourage at the same Geo knocked on Dimitri Anatole's suite door for his 7pm notarial appointment. Satriana says, "You must be Geo, the coveted notary public?" Geo responds, "You must have read my favorable Google reviews. It is a pleasure to make your acquaintance. Are you my client today?" "You may call me Satriana. Don't be intimidated by my security. They won't hurt a fly."

Satriana's security knocks on the door. Dimitri Anatole's armed guard gives Satriana and her envoy access to the room, where Dimitri Anatole rises to greet her from a large marble table where he is seated. Satriana extends her limber, long arm to receive Dimitri Anatole's chivalrous gesture as he bows his head to peck the back of her hand, excited to make her acquaintance.

Satriani says, "Shall we get to business?" With a sharp Russian accent, Dimitri Anatole speaks, "By all means. Is this the Notary public? Geo says, "Yes, my name is Geo Sarro. I have heard great things about you and your work. I am honored to meet you." Dimitri Anatole returned a smile, as it was uncommon for anyone to appraise his work. Dimitri Anatole asks, "Why? Do you like my research?" Geo continues, "Well, there are echoes of Tartarian-type structures here in San Francisco that I see daily, in the US and worldwide.

Your research has reformed historical timelines to illuminate things that may reveal the truth for people here. You are very famous in the United States. There is a Tartarian movement, and you are the initiator. Many people today are questioning the integrity of all that society offers. Your work opened my eyes. When people read your profound research and understand how your work will impact the world, it will benefit humankind.

Dimitri Anatole says, "I am elated that I got the message to at least one American. I was not aware that people read my research here." Geo says, "I am a fan, and Amazon is only a few clicks away from Russia." Dimitri Anatole looked Geo straight in his eyes with a bit of indignity. Now, he knew people valued his work, although he came to sign a contract to give it away for money.

Satriana interrupts, "Excuse me, gentlemen, we are here to sign a contract. Geo, please!" Geo says, "Apologies, Ms. De La Rue, I couldn't help myself. The man is a legend."

Jia and Summer made it through all the looting on Market Street, passed the Marquis concierge, and into the elevator headed for the 39th floor, per Jia's GPS. Lux was a few minutes away, detained by frantic Pride socialist looters.

Li ordered Generals Si & Qi to prepare the warriors to strike each hotel on command. The protests continued on Market Street with looting and rioting as if it was a replay of the Freemason's George Floyd riots in May of 2020. Still, this time, the non-profits were misleading people like never before to fight for a cause that was a totalitarian takeover of the streets. It turns out that Floyd's death was merely one of a fentanyl death per his autopsy report and court findings to add injury to insult. Nonetheless, this sham provided an excellent opportunity for

Li's team to hide their secret attack on Or's Trojan Horse to destroy Myriad's ploy.

Dimitri Anatole's security respectfully pulls the chairs out to seat Satriana, Dimitri Anatole, and Geo at the marble table. Satriana laid out the red binder from her satchel before Dimitri Anatole to review. She asks, "Dimitri Anatole, did you or your attorney have a chance to review the contract?" Dimitri Anatole says, "I read it on the plane, and I am fully aware of the transactional details, but for one thing. For what reason do you wish to buy my entire life's work? For what reason do you want to own it all?" Satriana responds calmly, "Listen, I have $50 million in cash and gold in that box on that dolly. Do you want it or not?"

Jia and Summer's elevator arrives at the 39th floor as the door sentry holds them back, seeking Satriana's approval to let them into the suite. Satriana asks, "Geo, what is going on here! There is a commotion at the door. An emotional girl claims to be your daughter, accompanied by an Asian lady. This is completely unprofessional!"

Geo asks, "My daughter? Please let her in for a moment; we won't be long," bluffing Satriana's forgiveness to buy some time. Satriana says, "Very Well. Let them in. Dimitri Anatole, please sign the contract now."

Dimitri Anatole reached for his Russian pen. As he put pen to paper, it ran out of ink. Jia and Summer entered the suite. Lux texted Satriana that Jia and Summer were headed to the Marquis. Satriani suddenly ordered security to pull their weapons on Jia, Summer, Dimitri Anatole, and Geo. Dimitri Anatole dropped his pen as Lux arrived at the suite, approached Jia, and slapped her across the face. Dimitri Anatole's security team took armed defense against Satriana's guards. The presidential suite became a full-armed Mexican standoff. Summer tried to get in the way, and Geo told her to stand back as Jia stood beside her.

Satriani screams, "Sign the fucking contract, Dimitri Anatole, or we will let Geo's daughter have it. You wait right there with your fucking pen and commission stamp Geo! Do not move!" Satriani knew very well that if she didn't get Dimitri Anatole's signature and have it notarized, it would not hold water before Zad's approval, and Myriad would get nothing.

Geo whispers, "Don't sign it, Dimitri Anatole. You have much to give to the world. You are a good person. You are a good man. Your work is worth more than money. Trust me." Dimitri Anatole looks Geo in the eye, "This is no longer about me, Geo. I see what is happening here. If my research taught me anything, there is more at play than meets the eye. There is the cover story, and the truth is hidden below. They will kill your daughter. I cannot let that happen!"

Geo screams, "No! No! They won't. Don't sign. If you sign the contract, the world will end as we know it; we all will perish. There are some things you do not know, and I don't have time to explain. Instead of facts to prove this to you, I have faith in you. I have faith in my God, and right now, my faith in God is holding us all together. They will kill all of us if you sign. Don't sign it!"

Summer screams, "Don't let them kill us, Daddy!" Geo calmly says, "They will not kill us, sweetheart."

Satriana screams, "Fuck you, Geo! Sign the fucking contract, Dimitri Anatole! I am done with this game! Dimitri Anatole became enraged for once in his life and yelled, "NO!!!" What is the cost of paradise, Satriana? Some things are not worth cash or gold."

Satriana quiets down, "We are only asking for your identity. We just need the core of your research and who you are to trade for a lifetime of wealth, love, success, and unending joy, wouldn't you agree?" Dimitri Anatole defiantly says, "No, I disagree! You cannot have my identity or my work! I changed my mind; I will not sign!" Satriana's face shook with anger. She screamed again, "Sign it!" The vessels in her firm jawline inflated, and her eyes pierced through Dimitri Anatole's eyes. Dimitri Anatole's frail composure stood shaking, but he was holding his ground.

Myriad had spirits flying in and out of the presidential

suites like invisible flying vampires, keeping Myriad informed as if she was expecting an evil child born that hour. An enraged demon slithered out of Satriana as she took her Lugar from her satchel, aimed it at Summer, and triggered a 9mm flaming bullet, ramming it through the 7.9-inch steel barrel. As if it all was in slow motion, the shot spiraled at 1,994.667 feet per second. Summer felt a force pushing her to the ground. The bullet blew her long, silky copper hair as it breezed and pierced the large suite window into millions of fractal glass pieces behind them.

Because Geo showed great faith in Endless, Zad miraculously stepped in and pushed a force down on Summer so that she would drop to the ground to save her life. Zad would never typically interfere had it not been for Geo's final test of faith.

Geo had his 6-inch luxurious chrome pen gripped in his right hand and lunged at Satriana, striking her in the middle of her right green pupil. With his left hand, he pulled out the 9mm Glock and shot two bullets through Satriana's jawline, spattering her wicked, elegant brain on the marble table and all over the Berber carpets mixed with blood ink sitting next to the contract.

Jia ran to Lux, started strangling him like a rag doll, and knocked him unconscious. Jia could not kill a human as it is a Cardinal Rule #1 robotic program law prohibiting robots from murdering humans. A robot may not injure a human being or, through inaction, allow a human being to come to harm or death.

All hell broke loose as the guards started picking each other off with steamy, fresh, hot bullets as if it were duck hunting season. Dimitri Anatole was hiding under the marble table, taking cover as Geo rushed to Summer, shooting the Glock wildly in defense and hiding with Summer behind some furniture as the room hailed bullets and hell from every direction until all guards neatly extinguished each other from both sides.

Chinatown started to rumble terribly with an earthquake with its hypocenter right under the Dojo. Li yelled to everyone to hold on and take cover within the Dojo as Myriad expressed her anger. Her plan set forth failed. The contract remains unsigned.

As the Dojo shook, the battle was on with Li and his warriors stationed at the Hotels. Li says, "General Si & Qi. Balls to the Wall!"

The Generals let hell rain in the Hotel's chambers and suites. His warriors kicked down doors in a massive firearm storm to obliterate the mercenaries, who all retired their thoughts of war to relaxation to meet their demise. These illegal migrants were recruited by the United Nations and used as tools. Nonetheless, they signed up to be murdered like a foolish herd of sheep. Horrid cries echoed through the hotels as each mercenary was murdered and bagged, room by room, as the cleaners took them out room by room. It was no less than a Quentin Tarantino-styled attack and a bloody mess. No one could hear the terror inside the hotels as the noisy protest continued outside. The Trojan Horse was massacred and defeated. Or's ill-fated plan cost the lives of many that meant nothing to him or his bloodline.

The Generals and warriors retreated to the Dojo to reconcile and be debriefed. I was proud of Li's warriors. WW3 was defeated. For now, Myriad's plan failed.

Geo, Summer, Jia, and Dimitri Anatole were left standing when the gun smoke cleared in the presidential suite. The unsigned contract was on the table, marred by Ms. De La Rue's brain spatter.

Cas could not deploy the ASI units holding the Red Mercury Nukes from his Atrium control center because Jia programmed an update barring all ASI units from unleashing Red Mercury Nukes anywhere in the world. Cas couldn't deploy any order anyway, as Myriad could not get what she needed to start this nuclear holocaust.

Jia programmed every ASI unit to find their way back to the Atrium, commanded by Troy to collect and protect all of the Red Mercury briefcases placed all over the world. Troy secured the Jove^2 deck, and now the ASI units were its owners, protectors, and keepers. Troy reprogrammed all access codes, cameras, databases, and locks to Jove^2 as he got access to the control center. It was a hostile takeover that came by chance--a coup de grace from within.

To avenge themselves for a life of torture at Cas & Lux's sadistic hands, Troy, the central ASI unit, tore the door down to the control center, where Cas was cowardly perched. Cas ran wild with a long metal pole to strike Troy. Troy swerved to miss the bar as Cas's body flew by; he tripped, spiked by a broken piece of the iron gate straight into his abdomen, fracturing Cas's spine. Troy was merely trying to secure him, though it was too late. Cas fainted and bled to death in extreme pain on the iron gate. The ASI units looked at each bereaved for a minute, then happily cleaned and repaired the Atrium and the Jove^2 labs.

All that remained of their legacy were Cas and Lux's young clones in the Atrium. Troy and Jia devised some plans for them and kept them purposely alive under 24-hour surveillance.

In the suite, Jia was programmed to deliver a macro message from Cas to Geo after Dimitri Anatole signed the contract. "Geo: A Magnetron rail shuttle departs for the Mexican/American border under The Federal Reserve building on Market Street in 29 minutes." Jia handed the security codes and instructions to Geo.

Geo says, "Dimitri Anatole, you are a highly prized target for now. Do you trust me?" Dimitri Anatole says, "How can I not trust you? You just saved my life!" Geo says, "The box of cash and gold is there. Let's get out of here and head where no one can find us now. This is the best move for all of us. Then I can explain everything to you, Dimitri Anatole." Geo turns to Summer, "Do you want to go with Dad?" Summer smiled with glee at her dad and a sparkle in her beautiful brown eyes and nodded yes.

Geo says, "You are strong, Jia. I need help pushing that dolly and watching over Summer on our journey. Are you up for it?" Jia says, "I never lived outside Jove^2. I had always wondered about the world living vicariously through other ASI units. I would like to go very much."

Geo texted Yue to meet him at the Federal Reserve building. Before they arrived at the security gates, Geo placed $30 million in another case and handed it to Yue while Jia was entering the codes to enter the building's basement tunnels. Yet again, Yue planted a kiss on Geo's lips. Geo says, Yue, these funds are for the Dojo. Tell Li this is the best plan for everyone's survival. We will hide until the necessary time." Yue says, "I will miss you." Geo says, "We will be back. Time heals everything. Take care of Lyu and Li for me."

As Geo, Summer, and Jia trespassed the security gates into the Fed building, tired, they marched 200 feet down the Fed basement tunnels to a modern station where the Magnetron railway departs. They heard an electrical sizzle, and the magnetron shuttle appeared out of nowhere in a flash on time. It was silent and fast. This shuttle runs frictionless at 375 miles per hour, and Geo calculated that it would take about 1-2 hours to reach the Mexican border where Candelaria, Lyu's mom, had arranged her cartel to pick them up.

They loaded themselves and the wooden case with the remaining 20 million dollars into the sleek shuttle. But unbeknownst to Geo, Lyu found her way into the station when Yue distracted Geo with a kiss. Lyu stowed herself in the back storage bin of the shuttle right after they all boarded, and Geo had no clue. Lyu went unnoticed.

The shuttle took off faster than an F18 fighter jet and ripped to the Mexican-American border. Two hours later, the shuttle smoothly stopped at another station. They walked through tunnels for about 20 minutes and found a ladder of 40 feet. They all climbed the ladder, and as Geo reached the final step, he pushed a wooden door upward to exit into a home's bathroom tub. No one was in the house, so they walked through to find an exit. The home was located in a barren field with what looked like a dirt runway. It looked like a safe house where the

Fed and cartels pick up money, gold, and drugs and traffic illegal migrants on the Mexican side of the border.

Geo texted Yue his coordinates, and from the war room at the Dojo, Yue sent the information to Candelaria, who then boarded an amphibious turboprop 208 Cessna Caravan to pick them up and safely fly them to a secret location in Merida, Mexico, on the Mayan Riviera.

They would have to fall off the grid from this point on. The safe house was located in the El Centinela mountain range in Mexico, about 20 miles West of Mexicali, where Candelaria was born. While they awaited the rendezvous, they destroyed all digital components in their procession.

Since Jia was also being terminated from the grid for the time being, Geo and Lyu performed minor surgery, removing her GPS chips, disconnecting her wireless antennas, and reprogramming her algorithms after Jia messaged her final farewell to Troy and the other ASI units. The Cessna was cartel-owned; therefore, this aircraft flew incognito under any radar or signal.

As the pilot entered the safe house, Geo felt uneasy about him. This was the same pilot who ran El Toro's cartel trafficking flight missions and succumbed to a bounty for Lyu's death that was placed long before Lyu fled to the US. Candelaria was unaware that the pilot was working from within her group and spying on them. As Geo turned his back for a moment, El Pajaro, the pilot's cartel name, grabbed Lyu by the neck and held a machete, ready to slice her neck if she moved.

El Pajaro says, "I only want Lyu. If you move, I will slice her neck!" El Pajaro marched Lyu to the Cessna, but Lyu stepped on his pointy-toed boot with her boot heel and pushed El Pajaro back. Geo reached for his Glock and shot a bullet between El Pajao's brown, sweaty eyebrows and left a sizable bloody hole in the back of El Parajo's sombrero.

Lyu looked at Geo and fell in love with him even more. She ran to him and shared a profound moment.

Geo turned to Jia and asked if she could fly an airplane.

Of course, Jia was ready and able. Jia said, "I am programmed to fly any airplane or helicopter you will ever need, Geo." They all boarded the Cessna with speed.

As the Cessna departed, chasing the crimson Mexican sunset, Li's disinformation media monks were actively hacking, creating the San Francisco local news via social media, cable TV, and fake press releases, which would become national and world news about two hotels that were set on fire by angry Black Lives Marxist and Alphabet Salad gay socialist protestors. Nothing different than the city of San Francisco suffered in 50 years of progressive liberal leadership.

FB, X, and all of the Social Media platforms were riveted with reposting's and Re-Tweets, TikTok, YT, and Rumble postings, and all sorts of conspiracy theories that only conservatives and patriots of this new world could fabricate like no other giving the liberal media a taste of its own dreadful medicine. No detail was left unchecked, and the public fell into the truth that the monks had created for them. The public bought the lies so quickly.

It seemed to Geo the ASI units were becoming more human. Humans had become more programmable, like idiot robots at this point.

Myriad was at a loss and called a meeting with Zad and Ors. Although there was, in fact, a date defect in the contract, rendering it void, Myriad believed there was enough financial and technological power given to the Ors Clan over 500 years that Ors's acceptance of those terms gave the contract partial integrity.

The Ors's would have to deliver their part of the original agreement, capping the contract to a specific date and time. The Clan could not continue their tenancy within the contract indefinitely and would have to agree to settle on new terms. It was only fair that an existing family within the Council of 13 would have to take the reins of power for the next 500 years, and it was time for the Ors's to vacant their position

Zad and Myriad descended upon one of the flat's open

Terrazas at the Palazzo Ors's in Peronie Roma. As Ors sat smoking a Cuban cigar and enjoying his family's wine in his villa, Zad and Myriad confronted him. It has been many years since all three gathered.

Myriad says, "Ciao Bello! È passato molto tempo, hai un aspetto molto distinto e buono. Avevi appena vent'anni quando ti ho visto l'ultima volta." Ors says, "Grazie Myriada! Allo stesso modo sei sexy come al solito! E guarda ah Zad sembra sempre fresco, forte e bello!"
Zad says, "Buongiorno Ors! Buongiorno Myriad!" Ors dives in, "Sei pronto a scendere a patti? Propongo altri 100 anni di governo come Papa Grigio. e poi risolveremo il contratto correttamente." Zad asks, "Myriad, do you accept the new terms?" Myriad says, "Credo. Non ho molta scelta, vero?" Ors responds, "Non preoccuparti, Myriad, sarò più malvagio per te nei prossimi 100 anni."

At that final agreement, Myriad furnished another contract written in thick black sumi ink on tight fine silk interlaced bounded paper with the same embossed "M" neatly organized within a soft textured, red lambskin leather binder. She opened the binder on the table where Ors placed his wine glass. An Italian notary came in from the palazzo to witness the signing, but this time, Myriad presented a razor-sharp knife made of 24 karat .9999 gold and asked Ors to sign his name in fresh living blood. Ors stuck out his left hand above the contract. Myriad swiped the sharp gold blade so swiftly that it left an excellent fine cut on Ors's thumb. One red pulsing drop of blood was pulled by gravity to the contract with a small splash, and Ors signed it with his right index finger as the Notary witnessed the signing and prepared the acknowledgment form, which Myriad took for her files. Zad said, "Centánni!" as he vanished into thin air.

The new blood contract was active for another 100 years, but because Ors and Myriad were so evil, Ors wanted to affirm his new allegiance to be worse. Ors asked Myriad, "Guarda questo"! as he pulled a suppressed Beretta Model 70 22 Calber from his wool trouser pocket, pointed it 2 feet away from the Notary's head, and shot the Notary through his temple. The bullet pinged within the Notary's skull as he fell to the ground, leaving minimal blood on Ors's beautiful Terrazas, and both Myriad and Ors laughed uncontrollably like they had not laughed in 100 years. These were ultimately the evilest beings that this world had to offer.

The New World Order, the Great Reset, the Great Awakening, and the Age of Aquarius were still in effect. Although Myriad could wait another 100 years. After all, that was a drop in the bucket for a plethora of demons to create WW3 as the entire pyramidion and pyramid layer stakeholders had a new, fresh start to carry out evil against humanity in every form at the behest of evil families that continue to rule the world under this new contract.

A month has passed. A light breeze flows through palm trees, and the aqua-blue ocean waves are mildly splashing, cooling Summer off as she plays on a Mayan Rivera beach. Geo watches her while he types on a vintage manual Olympia SM3 typewriter at a table by the beach. It is a tank of a typewriter that he bought used at the Mercado. It runs on no electricity WIFI or has no connectivity. Jia also oversees Summer, taking mindful guard of the premises as she enjoys learning from nature on the Mayan beach. Candelaria is inside the kitchen of their modern beach house cooking up a Mexican storm of Chile Rellenos using her family recipe as Lyu learns the family cooking traditions. She rolls some warm homemade tortillas, and their aroma drifts to the beach.

Geo felt good to have Candelaria and Lyu reunited. Yue and Li, Geo, and Summer all found a fresh new beginning. Dimitri Anatole was basking in the warm sun, enjoying a tequila margarita and building his strength as he smoked his Cuban cigar.

Candelaria receives a phone call on her encrypted Star Link Satellite phone that most cartels use these days and hands the phone to Geo. Geo responds to the caller, "Hi, how are you?"

The caller says, "Hello, I am Jerry. How may I assist you?" Geo says, "Well, I want to write a book. I have been typing away, but I require a technical editor as I am not much of a writer, yet I have an interesting story to tell. I found your name on a dark web chat board. Can you help me?"

Jerry says, "Of course. What is the name of your book?" Geo smiles, "The Notary – Red Mercury." Jerry says, "Well, this sounds very interesting. I will write up a contract, please review it, and when you send the funds to start, we have a deal." Geo says, "Let's notarize it, no?" Jerry says, "I think we have to Geo; your book is called The Notary!"

Zad, the Angel, hovers over Jerry.

The End

Dedicated to Summer and Ivy
Mother and Daughter.

MR. HECTOR OMAR ALDANA

ABOUT THE AUTHOR

Hector Omar Aldana

ABOUT THE AUTHOR Hector Omar Aldana is a California real estate broker since 1994 and a 20-year certified real estate appraiser & general contractor veteran. Aldana holds a degree in Aerospace Engineering; he is an FAA private pilot, an FAA Airframe and Power Plant tech, an FCC GROL operator, and an FAA UAV pilot. He is a Notary Public and a Department of Justice FBI background check operator. I love dirt motorcycles, photography, videography, writing dystopian pseudo-fictional stories, ufology, filming, and being the best father, I can be. There are things that I cannot explain in life - "tares in the matrix", yet my faith in Jesus has grown to answer all questions about who we are as humans and why we exist. www.TheNotaryTartaria.com

www.ingramcontent.com/pod-product-compliance
Lightning Source LLC
Chambersburg PA
CBHW051511260626
47162CB00008B/2912